I0717923

THREE SPACE OPERA ADVENTURES

STARFIGHTER
ORIGINS

M.G. HERRON

Copyright © 2023 by M.G. Herron. All rights reserved.

Cover art by Elias Stern.

Cover design by Miblart.

This is a work of fiction. Any resemblance to actual persons living or dead, businesses, events, or locales is purely coincidental. This story may not be reproduced without express written consent.

For Mom,

*Whose love and enduring support built me up and made it possible
to dream, even when the aliens abducted me at sixteen.*

With love, always,
Matthew

SPART PARTS

BOOK 1

ONE

Ever since they became refugees, Elya Nevers collected bot parts.

He didn't know exactly how the idea had first come to him. Even his memory of it as an idea was nebulous. Elya couldn't recall the concepts of *collecting* and *bot parts* ever pairing in his brain before they fled their cliffside solar farm in the night. He barely had time to throw a change of clothes and his tab into his rucksack before his mother dragged him and his two older brothers out the door and into the darkness. In their flight to the city, there had been no time for such thoughts.

He didn't remember making a conscious decision to be a collector when the four of them shoved their way onto an orbital transport shuttle, fighting against the panicked crowds, nor when the shuttle blazed through the planet's atmosphere. It was hard to focus on much of anything when the seat was rattling so hard he thought his brains would shake out of his mouth and splash all over his only pair of boots.

When they passed into space and the shuttle stabilized,

Elya looked down and noticed that his left hand was bleeding where he gripped a gold-tinted gear in his palm. Its reflective surface, even smeared with blood, calmed him for some reason. As he studied its finely cut teeth, noting its purposeful shape, he realized that he must have picked up the gear along the way, although he couldn't for the life of him remember where or when. Its golden color was distinctive compared to the dull grey of the utility bots they sometimes rented as extra hands to help during harvest time on the farm. Elya didn't really have a use for the gear, since the Nevers had never been able to afford a bot of their own—especially not a gold-plated one. *But I do have room in my rucksack*, he thought, and decided to keep it.

When the shuttle reached the limit of its range, the refugees were transferred to a Mammoth longhauler. Elya had plenty of time to contemplate his new habit of collecting bot parts during their harried spaceflight, while his mother clutched her bead necklace and muttered prayers under her steaming breath. When she finally slept, he and his brothers listened to their frightened fellow refugees speculate how long it would take the Imperial Fleet's starfighters to find them and guide them to safety. (Answer: twenty-three days, Galactic Standard Time.)

While they waited, the slow-moving longhauler drifted on minimum viable power—life support only. They kept the passenger cabin above freezing, but not by much, and the pilot had the ship's comms beacon off so that the Kryl couldn't track them. The only lights found among the stowaways were hoarded by the few people smart enough to pack electric torches, or wealthy enough to own personal servant bots in their previous lives. Elya had never seen luxury bots like these up close before, but he saw that only a few of them were finished in the same shade of gold as his gear.

He stayed warm by searching the passenger cabin for

more spare parts. The behavior became as much a part of him as his darkly tanned skin or his long, dextrous fingers. When he was alone in the dark, Elya would pass the time counting and cataloging his growing collection by feel. Since the gear, most of the spare parts he gathered had been found on the floor of the longhauler. Others he looted from a closet full of damaged Mammoth repair bots. Once, he won an aluminite power switch playing aleacc against a rich merchant's son. The stunned look on the kid's face when Elya rolled doubles three times in a row was his greatest source of pleasure on the seemingly endless journey. Elya placed the switch carefully in his rucksack. At night, when sleep wouldn't come, he would take it out and flip the mechanism back and forth, back and forth.

But nothing cleared or calmed his mind like the feel of the golden gear against his skin. It was the only thing he had left that reminded him of home.

<h1 style="text-align:center">TWO</h1>

An overwhelming stench struck Elya like a fist halfway down the airlock connecting the Mammoth long-hauler with the space station. The smell was sour and heavy and so thick it made him gag. He looked down and coughed, someone jostled him, and he staggered sideways under the weight of his pack.

His older brother caught him before he could fall. "Easy, little brother," Arn said.

Arn was the eldest of the three Nevers boys—tall and calm and always ready with a word of encouragement. Had those lines in his forehead always been etched so deep? Elya hadn't seen Arn's face in the light often during their space-flight, but he didn't think so. The ship's lights had only come on for the first time when the longhauler got clearance to dock with the space station. Elya's eyes had been adjusting to the overwhelming brightness ever since.

"Try breathing through your mouth," Arn said. "It still reeks, but you won't notice as much."

Elya nodded. He kept walking and tried not to vomit up the vitamins sitting like dead power cells on the floor of his hollow stomach. By pretending he didn't have a nose and keeping his eyes on Rojer's back instead of the vacuum of dead space on the other side of the transparent walls, he made it to the end of the airlock's gangway without puking.

It didn't take long to discover the source of the stench—a crowd of sweaty, unwashed people filled the vast hangar in which they emerged. They covered the floor, even spilling over into the demarcated area where smaller spaceships docked, unloaded, or refueled. At the far end from where they stood, an arched doorway led to the rest of the station. An enormous line trailed from that opening. Elya didn't need anyone to explain to him why it was so crowded; it was obvious: the space station's shuttle bay had been transformed into a refugee intake center.

Elya followed his brothers and his mother to a speck of empty floor where they wouldn't get jostled by the many moving bodies, or block the way of those still coming out behind them. The airlock they had come through was one of a dozen such mouths, each pouring out innumerable unkempt refugees from several different vessels—people from Yuzosix, just like them. Tens of thousands had already arrived and were making their vague way through the line— and then through the door that led to the rest of the station, and the end of this part of their journey. Elya didn't know what awaited them on the other side of that door, but almost anything was better than living in perpetual darkness on the Mammoth.

Elya's mother studied the crowd, then sighed. She looked each of her boys in the eye. "Stay close, all right? Watch out for each other."

"Where are we going now?" Rojer whined.

"They have to process us," Mom said. "To know how many people made it out." *Out alive. Out of Yuzosix.* "It shouldn't take long."

Arn nodded and smiled, to reassure their mother. It worked less well than it normally did. Elya scuffed a shoe against the floor. His mother smiled back, and it looked forced. Rojer continued to look sullen and angry—but that wasn't all that unusual.

Elya tightened the straps of his rucksack, then put his hand into his pocket and ran his fingers over the golden gear's teeth. Their hard edges, the satisfying way they rose and fell as he traced them, kept him from showing his anxiety to the rest of the Nevers clan.

"And you," Mom said, pointing a long bony forefinger at Elya so that he couldn't pretend she was talking to Rojer or Arn instead. "Don't wander off. We're not on the longhauler anymore. We don't know anything about these people, and I don't want to lose you."

She took another deep breath and sighed, more heavily this time.

Together, they waded into the sea of people. Mom led the way, with Rojer right behind her kicking at debris and vitamin wrappers on the floor. Elya came next, and Arn brought up the rear.

Not everyone seemed to be in the same rough shape as them. A large group accompanied by several security bots emptied luggage from small private ships to their right. Past them, a group of desert dwellers in brightly colored robes sat cross-legged on the floor around an oscillating hologram of a multi-armed deity who led them in prayer. A pair of old men whispered and passed a bottle between them, making faces as they swallowed. Most of the people he saw seemed to be from Yuzosix, but not all.

The less fortunate waited in a smaller line that formed fifty meters from the bigger one. Each person who got to the front was scanned for ID, and then doled out rations by a plump man in an Imperial uniform. He wielded a handheld holodisplay connected to the ship's main computer and an expression that reminded Elya of Rojer when someone stepped on his toes. The steward was flanked by two security guards of his own—human soldiers, not bots. These men and women bore blaster rifles in their arms, and attentively studied the people in line. Like the steward, their uniforms were a rich blue trimmed in crimson. Similarly uniformed guards, each wearing a helmet that concealed their face, were spaced out around the edge of the hangar.

As they walked, Elya's attention was drawn like a magnet to a third small theater that had formed in a far corner of the hangar. People there weren't lined up so much as gathered around, shoulder to bot to shoulder. Everyone waiting in the crowd had a decommissioned bot either held in their arms or wheeled on a maglev dolly at their side. A few of the personal servant bots were standing and operational, but most were not.

Everyone seemed to be vying for the attention of a giant man in a red jumpsuit. He had enormous muscular arms and shoulders, and long dark hair gathered with rubber bands into thick ropes. The man lifted his muscular arms and rained three blows down on something that echoed with a hollow metallic gong each time he struck it. He switched the tool in his hand, slapped a mask down over his face, and touched the flame of a welding torch to the object; an explosive hiss reverberated into the hangar's high ceilings. As people waiting jostled and shoved for prime spots near the front of the gathering, Elya caught a glimpse of the bot he was working on—a personal servant bot finished in red-tinted silver. The tristar Imperial insignia was painted in black on the bot's chest.

"Watch it, runt!" Rojer snapped, shoving Elya sideways. Rojer was always calling Elya names, but this time he thought he might have actually deserved it. Elya had been so caught up studying the machinist and the anxious crowd that had gathered to take advantage of his talents that Elya didn't notice he had bumped into his brother.

But even if he was in the right, Elya hated it when Rojer was mean to him. Rojer hadn't seemed to have the heart to be nasty on the longhauler, where there was no light and no one knew if they would be rescued or starve to death as they drifted through space. Here, in the light and noise of the space station, it was different. Rojer felt emboldened. Heads snapped toward them, and under the weight of hundreds of eyes, Elya felt his face flush with shame.

"Cut it out, both of you," Arn snapped. He stepped between them, trying to defuse the situation. The smirk on Rojer's face caused Elya to see red. He knew what Roj was thinking: *Arn to the rescue*. Well, not this time.

He lunged around Arn and grabbed Rojer by the thick curls their mother loved so much. Yanking down, he was glad to hear his brother shout in pain and fright, and flail about, slapping at Elya's wrists. But he had his long fingers gripped tight about his brother's hair, and the pain he felt at his brother's blows wasn't nearly as scary as it used to be. Not after their flight from Yuzosix. That experience had reset his pain tolerance to a new plateau in ways Elya was only now, in this moment, coming to understand.

One of Rojer's flailing arms caught Elya's rucksack, and he managed to pull so hard that Elya stumbled forward. Hair ripped, Arn shouted, and Elya pitched to the ground, scraping his chin against the rough metallic floor of the hangar.

He fully expected the weight of his pack to crush the wind from his chest, or perhaps protect him from Rojer as his brother fell on his back, but neither of those things happened. Instead, his pack felt light as air. A musical tinkling sound made Elya's blood run cold.

Lifting his head, Elya watched in helpless horror as the contents of his rucksack tumbled forth, between the legs and under the feet of the crowd. Not just blankets and his toothbrush and dirty underwear, but the bot parts he'd so secretively and carefully stowed. Nuts and bolts scattered and fell between cracks in the floor. Tubes and wires were stomped underfoot and ground down. A ball bearing met the toe of a shoe at speed and rocketed away, lost forever in a dense patch of people to his right.

Worst of all, the golden gear fell out of his pocket, and momentum set the precious piece to rolling. It wobbled as it found its balance, then came upon a slight slope and rolled away, nimbly dodging between pairs of legs whose owners Elya couldn't see and didn't care to know.

He realized by then that Rojer's flailing arms must have caught the zipper and opened his pack, but Elya only had eyes for the gear. He struggled to his knees, having forgotten all about Rojer until a sharp pain blossomed against the back of his skull, and a weight from above tried to smear him across the grated metal flooring of the hangar.

"Get off!" Elya shouted, "Rojer, getoffame!"

"I didn't know you were such a packrat, Elly."

Though it took all the air left in his lungs, Elya cried, "Don't call me that, you sniveling little twerp!"

"*Elya!*" his mother screeched, as she finally noticed what was happening behind her. How she could be more alarmed about Elya's choice of words than his short-tempered and obnoxious brother attacking him for no reason was beyond him. His mother's abiding love and forgiveness of Rojer's insufficiencies was one of the Seven Galactic Wonders.

Arn set his feet on either side of Elya's head, balled Rojer's clothes in both of his huge hands, and hauled their brother bodily into the air with a roar of effort. Rather than face his mother or watch Rojer be manhandled by Arn—as much pleasure as that *always* gave him—Elya scrambled to his feet and ran in the direction the gear had gone. He never took his eyes off it. The gear rolled with beautiful efficiency, its finely cut teeth allowing it to tumble unheeded over the hangar floor.

The golden gear turned between the legs of a boy, who missed his chance at grabbing it, and then beneath the frayed skirts of an old lady before it finally fetched up against a rubber sole of someone's boot.

The boot attached to the rubber sole was made of expensive, oiled leather. Tucked into their fur-lined tops were clean, crisply ironed pants—made of the expensive fiber the Nevers family had grown in their solar farm, to sell to the merchants in Yuzo City. As Elya's eyes traveled up, he realized that the expensive boots and pants belonged to the merchant's son, the same snot-nosed brat he'd won the power switch from in a game of aleacc onboard the Mammoth. He had known the kid was taller than him, but now that he was properly lit and standing next to a gleaming golden servant bot, Elya saw that the boy was older than Elya by at least a few years, and well-muscled in ways that Elya's body, just barely edging into puberty, was not yet even capable of becoming.

With a smirk like a dull knife, the merchant's son caught Elya's forlorn gaze, then bent down and picked up the gear. The boy twisted the golden cog in the light. Then, without breaking eye contact, he placed it inside his tunic, next to his skin.

Elya's fists tightened into balls. This boy had a servant bot of his own. What in all the livable worlds did he need with a lonesome gear? Besides, that gear belonged to Elya. He'd found it, so it was his by rights. More importantly, it came from Yuzosix, so it had more sentimental value than all the other parts he'd collected put together. Elya shoved his way through the crowd, ignoring the sounds of scratching and arguing coming from Arn, who was still tangled up with Rojer, and ignoring his mother's cries as she tried to pull the two apart.

Elya closed the distance to the merchant's son in a few quick strides.

As it became apparent where Elya was headed, the servant bot stepped forward and put himself between Elya and the snot-nosed boy, whose name was... What was his name? Elya couldn't remember. It didn't matter.

"That's mine," Elya said, pointing an accusing finger at the boy's tunic where he had tucked the gear away.

"What is?" the boy said, touching an artistic hand to his chest and putting on his best confused face.

Elya barely recognized the fury seething through his bones and causing him to curl his toes in his boots. Words shot straight from his aching heart to his tongue, bypassing his brain completely. "You know what," Elya growled.

The boy looked around, then up at the bot. "I really don't. Do you, Ambit?"

The bot cocked its head and glanced between the two of them. "I am no longer certain, Master Kristoph."

Oh, that's right. The boy had introduced himself as Kris when they played aleacc together on the Mammoth. "Kris, please... I—I need that back."

"Or what?" he asked, his tone mocking.

"I just need it back."

Kristoph shrugged. "Not my problem," he said, dropping the feigned ignorance now that it no longer benefited him. "You have one of mine, and now I have one of yours. It seems to me like we're even."

"I won that power switch fair and square, and you know it. You didn't win the gear. You just stole it. It's not yours!"

Kristoph shrugged and studied his perfectly buffed nails.

How had this rich brat managed to stay so *clean* on the Mammoth, when Elya felt as if he'd been covered in a layer of dirt for a month? "Finders keepers."

This sent Elya into a rage, partly because he used the same justification to keep the gear in the first place. But there had been no encounter with the gear's owner when he discovered it. For all Elya knew, the golden gear had materialized out of thin air. It was just *there*, in his hands, absent of any question of ownership. Elya had felt like it belonged to him the first moment he laid eyes upon it and was careful to keep it private so that no such questions arose. By the time they were clear of the planet's atmosphere, the gear really was his. There was no possibility of finding the owner. It was his by rights. Finders keepers.

Powered by this sudden anger, Elya leaped forward to snatch the gear straight out of Kristoph's tunic. But the servant bot was faster. A golden arm shot out, acting like a barricade that kept Elya at a safe and harmless distance.

Someone screamed. Only after bruising his knuckles and chipping his fingernails clawing and thrashing at the bot— and failing to gain so much as a centimeter—did Elya realized the animal noise was coming from his own throat.

"What is the meaning of this?" A fat, bearded man with a triangular hat bellowed, marching up from behind Kristoph.

"I don't know, father," Kristoph said. "This underfed gutter rat attacked me for no reason. If Ambit wasn't here…"

"Guards!" The man bellowed. "Guards!"

Elya froze. Guards were bad. Guards were real bad. *Where did Arn and Rojer go? Mom?* Looking around, he saw nothing but a sea of strange faces crowded tightly around, watching the drama unfold with cruel anticipation. In the distance, two blaster-wielding soldiers peeled away from the wall and began to wade through the crowd in their direction.

Feeling pressured as he saw his window of opportunity

closing, Elya became indignant. "He stole my gear. I'm just trying to get it back."

"Gear?" Kristoph's father, the merchant, demanded in a brusque manner, crossing his arms and glaring at his son. "Is this true?"

"What?" Kristoph scoffed. "No, of course not."

"I don't see any gear, boy. You're a liar."

"No!" Elya felt his face heat up. "No, I'm not. That's not true. He's the liar!"

At the insult to his son, the older merchant's broad forehead smoothed out. His face went stony and his arms dropped to his side.

"Ambit, down," the merchant said in a flat voice.

The golden bot dropped his arms to his side and made an electronic wheezing sound that came out like a sigh. His head dipped, almost as if he felt slightly guilty—Elya made that same gesture himself when his mother grilled him about something he shouldn't have been doing—then straightened.

Elya braced himself. But the blow he expected never came.

"Little brother," Arn said. The relief in his voice was palpable. "Come on, Elya. You can't keep wandering off like that."

"I didn't wander off!" Elya snapped. The indignation that had built up in the frustrating conversation with Kristoph spilled out all over his brother. He didn't mean to get angry at Arn, but it wasn't right. Arn smiled down at him sadly, as if at someone mentally inadequate. It filled Elya with both shame and confusion because he wasn't inadequate. That was Rojer, if it was anyone.

Before Elya could say anything else, his mother appeared, all smiles and apologies. "Please forgive my son," she said. "It's been a long journey, sir, and we're all very tired."

The merchant's face softened at the sight of his mother.

Elya noticed the way the man's eyes traveled up and down her body. He relaxed and smiled broadly. "It's no trouble."

"Thank you, sir," she said. "We'll be going now."

Arn slowly backed away, dragging Elya with him.

"But he stole my gear!"

"Quiet."

"But—"

"Shh!"

The rich merchant turned to talk to the guards, who had finally arrived, shrugging elaborately and laughing in his belly. Elya couldn't hear his words, but his expression seemed to say, *Boys will be boys, you know?* The guards followed the Nevers clan with their eyes but didn't pursue them.

Elya had no choice. He followed Arn and was shepherded along by his mother. When they got back to where Rojer was waiting, he was holding Elya's pack. It had been repacked with his belongings and what bot parts Rojer had been able to retrieve from the floor nearby. Elya snatched the rucksack out of his brother's hands and didn't speak to anyone for a long time.

THREE

After three days, Elya barely noticed the stink of unwashed people anymore, at least not unless he accidentally got up close to one. And he tried very hard to avoid that.

The space station was shaped like a star, five arms of five levels each. It was called Solaran's Bridge on the Imperial starmap Elya found on his tablet, and the cyclopedia described it as a pit-stop between the Yuzo chain of star systems and the viridian spiral arm. Or it used to be. Imperial newsfeeds all reported that the Fleet had pulled back to safety after the rescue. The volume of space between Yuzosix and Yuzotwelve was under Kryl control now. So, Elya supposed, Solaran's Bridge was no longer a pit-stop to anywhere people were safe. He wasn't afraid to admit how glad he was that the plan was to relocate his family, eventually. Their journey wasn't over quite yet.

For now, the Nevers were given a cramped little room in the corner of what Elya thought of as the north point of the star. In space there was no north, no true direction at all. It simply felt like that because of the way the design of interlocking arrows on the floor all pointed in a single direction. "It's so you always know where you are, and never get lost," Mom explained.

"I don't get lost," he insisted.

"It's still good to know," she said.

Arn insisted that Mom slept in the bottom bunk, while the boys rotated between the top bunk and the floor. The room was a cramped closet compared to the space they once shared in their cliffside dwelling—and certainly less room than Elya needed to get a break from Rojer's constant, low key torment—but it was more than they had on the Mammoth, and at least it had lights and a door that closed. For that, he was grateful.

Rumor had it that the researchers and staff had started to refer to the station as Solaran's *Ditch*, especially the lower levels given over to the refugees. To Elya, the halls seemed less crowded than the hangar, yet it became known that a hundred thousand people were currently breathing the same recycled air.

Even knowing the odds, it still took several days of searching for Elya to admit that his chances of recovering his golden gear had gone to zero. Despite seeing phantoms of Kristoph's dull-knife smirk around every corner, the merchant's family must have been able to afford quarters in a better part of the station than the Nevers. Though Elya kept his eyes peeled, he never saw the other boy.

He blamed Kristoph for stealing the gear, of course. And Rojer too. But he blamed himself most of all. After Yuzosix, Elya should have known better than to let himself get attached to anything.

As they were getting ready for bed one night, Rojer whined, "How long do we have to stay here?" Rojer got to have the bed the previous night. Now that it was Arn's turn, he was acting like a baby about it.

"Not long," Mom said. "This is temporary."

"Temporary until when?"

"Until they find a place to resettle us."

"I hope it's in the viridian spiral arm," Arn said. "I heard they have settler's moons there. Imagine if we were granted land to start a new farm." Of the three boys, Arn enjoyed farming the most. He found a quiet joy in hard labor that Elya never managed to muster. Arn was tall and strong, and even back on Yuzosix every commented on how his lanky frame had begun to gather muscle. He looked just like their father, people said. Compared to Arn, Elya was a runt. He was built more like their mother, quick and dextrous, but small and lean.

Rojer snorted. "And you know what they say about the girls on settler's moons."

"Stop it, Rojer," their mother chided, but Arn was already blushing.

Due to the influx of refugees on the station and the scarcity of essential supplies, food and water continued to be strictly rationed. Elya managed to save enough of his drinking water to wash himself over the sink every couple days. It wasn't the same as taking a hot shower, but it was better than smelling himself all the time. He wished Rojer would do the same. His brother had always hated washing up, and Elya was still too mad at him to give him the dignity of letting him know how badly he reeked.

Unlike his sour middle brother, Elya was determined to make the most of their stay. The station was packed to the gills with refugees from his homeworld, and there was a lot to see. Yuzosix had been a big planet and he'd only ever seen a small corner of it, so many of the people he passed in the halls appeared foreign to him. They dressed in different styles of clothing and spoke in dialects he'd never heard before. All the exotic wonder they represented made Elya restless. Fortunately, once the Nevers settled in, his mother gave him more slack to wander.

Under one condition. Arn had to accompany him; only then was Elya allowed to explore.

Arn rolled his eyes in front of Rojer, but he went willingly enough. After all, Rojer hadn't been wrong about their responsible big bro. A hundred thousand exotic people meant exotic women, and Arn wanted to meet them all.

It didn't take long for Elya to fill up his rucksack with newly discovered treasures. He had a talent for spotting bot parts. A small glint on the floor caught his eye while they were strolling along a corridor in the southeast corner of the station.

"What's that one?" Arn asked.

Elya picked it up, noting the evenly spaced lines along the outer rim of the circular knob. "Some kind of dial. You know, like the kind that might go on the outside of a servant bot's…" Elya trailed off and made a pulling gesture at his hip. "Container thingy."

"Cargo pocket?"

A snort tickled Elya's nose. "That's not what they're called."

"It's a pocket for cargo, isn't it?"

"If you say so." Elya had seen a bot struggling with such a compartment in its lower torso in this area of the station yesterday. Maybe the piece fell off of him. They were at the southeast point of the star, third level from the top. That bot had a knob just like the one. In fact, now that he gave it some thought, he'd found more odds and ends in the southern and eastern parts of the station than in other arms of the star. Only just now had his mind assimilated that information and recognized the pattern.

"What's that way?" Elya asked, pointing right at an intersection of two corridors. The chevron pattern on the floor angled left.

Arn scratched at his head. "I think that would take us to the hangar."

"Huh. I don't remember coming through this way."

"Me either. That first day was a blur."

After the encounter with Kristoph, Elya had endured the hours-long wait with a low fire of rage smoldering within him. The fury made his hands shake like an earthquake, so much so that his mother asked him if he was okay three or four times before she let him be. The anger sapped his strength and energy and soon his feet ached. After being stuck on the longhauler for three weeks, it had been an excruciating experience to stand for an entire day on a metal floor, shuffling slowly through the processing queue, in such an emotionally unstable state. By the time they were cleared and a pair of guards led them to their new room, the encounter with Kristoph had become like a bad dream. It haunted him, and he questioned all that had transpired.

The memory of this fugue state evaporated when a metallic gong echoed faintly down the corridor. Elya inhaled sharply and lifted his head. The sound was the mental equivalent of getting cold water splashed on his face. "Did you hear that?"

Arn frowned and shook his head. Elya waited. An elderly couple carrying shopping bags, then a gaggle of teenagers, passed them in the narrow hall, filling the air with giggling and whispers. Arn and Elya stood to the side and waited until they all passed.

Gong.

Arn grinned. "I heard it that time."

The prospect of a treasure hunt already had Elya's feet flying. "This way!"

He ran down the hall, right at the intersection, then

banked left into a sliding door, which retracted as he approached. As he passed through, the temperature dropped twenty degrees. They entered a large room lined with floor-to-ceiling shelves of vat-grown meats and cheeses, each separated by transparent panes of aluminite and individually temperature controlled. They had stumbled on a grocer's freezer. Each drawer was labeled with the name and logo of the producer. Judging by the notes, most of them were based on this station.

Elya and Arn passed through the grocery to an enormous hall beyond, which was honeycombed with dozens more shops of all kinds. They soon discovered that the honeycomb wrapped around the main hangar like a crescent around a moon. The walls and vaulted ceilings were all made of the same airy, 3d-printed foam material, cut with curved edges and supported by arch-like structures that lined the hall like the ribcage of some giant ocean monster. As a waystation between major star systems, it made perfect sense that Solaran's Bridge would need to be outfitted and supplied by a multitude of workers and goods. Elya had simply never thought through what that meant. In this area, people wearing the blue-grey uniforms of Solaran's Bridge staff ran about, busy as bees, while customers in a rainbow of brightly colored tunics, wearing soft shoes that would be no better than house slippers on Yuzosix, did their shopping.

The sound of the metallic gong grew louder as its ringing became less urgent. Elya knew he'd heard the sound before, but he wasn't sure until he caught sight of the huge dread-locked man. The top half of his red jumpsuit now hung loose around his lean waist. Over the ropy muscles of his huge arms and barrel chest, he wore a tank top that clung sweatily to his frame. The man gave the metallic shell he was working on one last adjustment, banging out the remainder of a dent with a big hammer. Then he grabbed a rag hanging from his waist and buffed out a few marks before placing the shell over the complex innards of some kind of low-slung utility bot. It had a dozen kinds of brushes embedded in its base, so Elya figured the bot was some kind of cleaning machine. He fleetingly wondered if it could do much to combat the stench of unwashed refugees.

The man flipped a power switch hidden on its undercarriage and the bot whirled to life. It spun in circles, buzzed and beeped proudly, then zoomed around the shop, leaving a debris-free trail in its wake that was noticeable in the messy shop. Elya couldn't help but smile at the little bot's antics. A big grin split the machinist's face as well, somehow softening his image and making him seem approachable in Elya's eyes.

The man looked up and seemed to notice them for the first time. "How can I help you?"

"Uh," Elya stuttered. Now that the man's attention was on him, he suddenly felt self-conscious. His eyes darted around, looking for a reason to be here. A hand-painted sign strung along the back wall had *Welcome to the Chop Shop!* scrawled across it in red paint, to match the man's red jumpsuit. "I just… wondered…"

"My little brother loves bots," Arn said. Elya swallowed his stuttering attempt at a greeting, thankful for his big brother's smooth intervention.

The machinist in the red jumpsuit stepped forward, running the grease-spotted towel over his meaty paws. His eyes lit up as he came to some sort of epiphany, then reached out a hand. Elya allowed his own hand to be swallowed in the machinist's. "I recognize you," the man said. "From the hangar last week, during the big intake. It was a lucky thing they found your Mammoth. Drifting out there without comms, hiding in the darkness. You got real lucky." When he shook his hand, Elya felt as if his whole body was being pumped up and down.

He nodded. "Yeah."

"I'm Cormorant. You can call me Core. Hell of a thing y'all had to go through. I admire how you've bounced back so quickly. Some aren't so fortunate."

Elya hadn't really considered how his own resilience played a part, but Core had a good point. Elya thought of Rojer, who was bottling up more anger at the world than he ever had before.

"If you're not a refugee," Elya said, "what were you doing in the hangar that day?"

"Just helping out. I've got a skill that people are sorely in need of, especially during hard times. Doesn't harm me none to turn a wrench for free for a little while. Besides, there's been plenty of business since, from those who can afford it. It helped get the word out. I've been going nonstop since you got here." His smile tilted toward his right cheek, giving him a roguish look.

The taste of Elya's encounter with Kristoph was still bitter on his tongue. At the mention of 'those who can afford it', Elya looked over his shoulder, expecting to see the dull-knife smirk lurking behind him... but it was just his imagination as usual.

Core turned away and grabbed a circular canister off a neat tool bench. He grabbed a pinch of something brown and stuffed it in his cheek as a teenage girl came around the corner into the front of the shop with her arms full of pipes and wires and other bot parts. They were piled so high she couldn't see where she was going and as she bumped into Arn, the pile teetered. She gasped as they fell.

"Oh," she yelped. "Sorry! I'm so sorry!"

"It's okay," Arn said, smiling his broad, affable smile as he bent down to help her pick up the pieces.

Arn could charm a powered-down bot with that smile if he tried hard enough. Elya rolled his eyes. The girl was near

Arn's age and cute in a clumsy sort of way, with long blond hair braided to the middle of her back. Arn was already lovestruck. His older brother whispered something that caused the girl to laugh and roll her eyes at him.

Several cases of new and refurbished bot parts drew Elya's attention away from them. There were power switches, bolts, dials, knobs. Touchscreen and hologram projectors. Plates with the Imperial insignia on them. A whole basket contained about six bazillion different kinds of wheels. Another case showed off magnets for a variety of uses, half of which Elya couldn't even fathom. His eyes fell on a tool chest where different sizes and types of gears were spread out. His breath caught in his chest at the sight of a few of the gold-tinted ones. Somehow, it was comforting to know that there were more gears like the one Kristoph had stolen out there in the galaxy. Even if he couldn't have them.

In a corner, in a plastic case that featured a biometric lock on the top, were hundreds of carefully stored power cells and processors—the most treasured and expensive parts of the bots, if he was to believe the price lists he found on his tab the other day. He bit his lip and sighed. No matter how badly he wanted those pieces, he couldn't afford them and he wouldn't dream of stealing them from Core even if he could. It was one thing to gather spare parts from the floor of the station, to recover castoffs that other people had lost or left behind. It was quite another to take something that wasn't his, especially from a professional bot machinist who relied on them to make his living.

But, oh, how he wanted one…

Elya forced his eyes away from the locked case to a poster hanging on the back wall. Not one of the holograms that normally decorated the walls of a house or shop, but the old-fashioned kind made out of some sort of printed polymer. The poster showed a pilot standing next to his starfighter, sweat streaking his face and grinning with his helmet gripped in the crook of his elbow. The man had a tristar insignia on his chest, the mark of the Solaran Empire and the Fleet. Char marks and debris scars decorated the front of the sleek plane behind him. A spider-like bot that came up to his knee was bouncing next to the pilot. The camera caught the bot in mid-jump, giving both he and the pilot a jubilant air.

"Good man, Captain Omar Ruidiaz," Core said. Elya hadn't heard the big man walk up behind him, but when he spoke Elya didn't jump. His voice was soothing. "We served together in the war. I learned my way around the inside of a bot as a starfighter mechanic while he flew his first missions."

Elya noticed the wistful tone in Core's voice. But only one thing interested him at this point. "Do all starfighter pilots have a bot of their own?"

"The smart ones do," Core said, "Fleet doesn't issue them, but if a bot meets the requirements they'll let a pilot bring them on missions. That one Ruidiaz built himself. With my help, of course."

Elya stared at Core, eyes lingering on the bulge of tabac stuffed into the man's cheek and the spark of mischief gleaming in his eyes. He realized that Core probably intimidated most people with his size. For some reason, Elya felt comfortable around the man. Something occurred to him, something he'd heard on the news or read on the cyclopedia somewhere.

"I thought most starfighters were operated remotely."

"No way. In the Yuzo chain, where you're from, maybe some are. It's a peaceful system… or it used to be." Elya pretended he hadn't heard that part. Core cleared his throat. "But on the front lines, you can't afford to rem-op a starfighter. Every nanosecond counts. Out there, a little lagtime can make the difference between life and death.

That's why the job is volunteer only. Starfighter pilots need to be able to make peace with putting their lives at risk."

Core stopped talking and turned to a viewscreen nearby. He waved it on with a gesture, flipped through a file structure to find what he was looking for. The same starfighter Ruidiaz stood next to on the poster was suddenly twisting around a Kryl drone like a kamikaze maniac, doing barrel rolls and turns that made Elya's stomach lurch and twist. Everyone had heard the stories about starfighter pilots defending against the Kryl when they first encountered Solaran exploratory vessels a century ago. The war had been such a distant thing from his home on Yuzosix… but not anymore. Now it had become personal, and suddenly Elya wanted very badly to be in the cockpit of a starfighter himself, doing barrel rolls around Kryl drones and blasting their motherships to smithereens alongside Captain Ruidiaz and his spider.

To the stars with risk.

"Easy, kid," Core rumbled.

Elya slowly unclenched his fists. His breath was coming fast. Crescent-moon marks in his palms stung where his nails had dug in. He realized he hadn't been picturing a pinched Kryl face, but Kristoph's dull-knife smirk, in his mind.

"Listen," Core said. "I saw what happened in the hangar with that merchant's kid. I can't give back what he took from you… but maybe this will help."

Core stepped back behind the sales counters and reached down beside the locked case of power cells and processors. The spiky metal object he picked off a bottom shelf fit in the palm of his meaty fist. Elya felt his breath quickening again, this time with excitement and anticipation instead of anger. Core reached out and Elya felt himself instinctively open his hands—his heart caught in his throat.

It turned out to be a bot. Not a spare part or a discarded knob, but an *actual* bot! The miniature machine transformed before his eyes, expanding to twice its original size as its legs unfolded and its body unfurled, turning from a spiky metal ball to a small hedgehog. Elya realized Core must have activated the bot as he dropped it into his hands. The spikes were actually hundreds of hair-thin polymer bristles, and it seemed to sniff his palm as Elya squatted down to set it gently on the floor.

"It can smell?" he asked.

"In a sense. Every bot is purpose-built. This one was designed to detect danger in hostile new environments. First, it takes a sample of your DNA. Then, it can test anything it encounters against your genetic code—other materials and objects, plants, liquids, even gases. The Fleet uses them on missions of planetary exploration to measure atmospheric composition, detect poisons in the water supply, that sort of thing."

The hedgehog explored outward from Elya, "sniffing" around him in ever-expanding circles. It was so quick, Elya felt like he could only track the bot in frames. A blue underglow trailed wherever it went so that Elya had no trouble following him when it disappeared into the back of Core's shop and crawled beneath a curved aluminite plate. When the hedgehog completed his exploration and returned to Elya, its lights blinked green three times. Elya bent down and let the bot crawl back into his hand.

"Green means all clear. If it blinks red, that's when you need to watch out." Core winked at him from his full, towering height. "You can read more about these models on your tab. Model number CL-454."

Elya nodded mutely and turned his rapt attention back to the tiny bot. It didn't seem real, to hold a bot of his very own in his hand. *CL-454. A hedgehog bot. Hedgebot.* All of a sudden, a guilt complex overwhelmed him. He held the bot out to Core. "He belongs to you. I can't afford to buy him."

"Nah," Core scoffed, "Don't sweat it. I've got enough bots to take care of. You take care of that one for me, okay?"

Elya nodded dumbly and swallowed against a dryness in his throat. He was overwhelmed—by the idea of having his own bot for the first time, by Core's generosity, by the tragedy that had upended his life and his family. It took a tremendous effort to hold the tears back so this man he respected, this generous stranger, didn't see him cry.

He kept his face turned away while nodding emphatically and cupping the tiny bot to his breast. Core seemed to understand, and went back to his work repairing bots beneath the *Welcome to the Chop Shop!* sign.

Arn was deep in conversation with the girl. She had put her arms back through the sleeves of a tan jumpsuit. The garb, along with the bot parts she had been caring, cemented the fact that she worked for the burly machinist. Maybe she was his apprentice. Elya burned with questions for her, about what it was like to work with bots.… but his brother was obviously enamored with the girl, hanging onto her every word while he wore a rapt expression Elya only saw on Arn's face under one condition.

Elya decided to give them some space.

Saying nothing, he turned and wandered out of Core's store, curious what else this honeycomb of shops had to offer. He held his breath, waiting for Arn to call after him, to warn him not to wander too far. The warning never came. Elya carried Hedgebot past an Imperial bank terminal, then by a dry goods store, then a weapons dealer, before he decided to experiment and set Hedgebot down for a bit. The mechanical creature surged ahead. Elya smiled helplessly as he followed the little bot through the halls. He noticed that Hedgebot never moved more than about twenty meters apart from him. Elya would have to do some research to find out if that was programmed in, and if he had any control over the length of the invisible tether. Despite this ineresting observation, his heart leapt into his throat when Hedgebot disappeared around a corner and behind a set of stairs.

There was a hidden storage area tucked away back here, a nook with no door where a bunch of lightweight folding chairs and extra tables had been stacked against the wall. But that was not what initially caught Elya's attention. Hedgebot had stopped just under the stairway, at the mouth of an open door. The halo of light around the bot had darkened to yellow and was slowly burning toward a red-tinted orange.

It only took a moment to see why. Elya froze. He didn't dare breathe and it was a good thing his new bot didn't have to. At the back of the storage room, three boys Arn's age surrounded a humanoid bot with a golden casing. One of the boys had a dull-knife smirk that was currently separated into a sharp-edged grin of maniacal proportions. This time the sight wasn't Elya's imagination or his mind playing tricks. It was Kristoph, in the flesh and blood.

The three boys didn't immediately notice Elya or his little danger-scouting Hedgebot for two reasons: One, Elya crouched in the shadow of the staircase. And two, they were too busy abusing the bot trapped between them to look around.

When Elya's mind snapped back into action, he came to his senses and took three steps backward, out of Kristoph's line of sight.

"Hedgebot!" Elya whispered. "Come back!"

The hedgehog twisted its head to look back at him, but didn't move away from the doorframe. Its underglow darkened another shade.

Elya felt his heart slam repeatedly into his ribcage. His

chest expanded and contracted rapidly. His palms, splayed against a metallic wall, left sweaty streaks where he pressed.

"Master, I do not understand," a servant bot's familiar electronic voice pleaded in a worried tone. The bot sounded distraught.   A metallic crunch reverberated through the cracked door. This time it wasn't the siren call of the Chop Shop, but a clamor far more sinister.

"Shut up, Ambit," Kristoph snapped.

A hollow thump sounded as someone struck the bot again. Elya flinched at the sound.

"Your father would not approve." Ambit scolded Kristoph as if he were a child. Such a tone would have worked on Elya.

"I said, *shut up!*" This time the noise was not a simple thud, but a *rip-tear-crunch*.

Ambit did not respond. The silence was deafening. Still frightened, but now filled with a terrible curiosity, Elya ventured a peek around the corner. Ambit's arm lay on the floor. The gold-skinned servant bot bent to retrieve it. He slowly picked up his arm and gazed at it with a cocked head, as if something was severely out of order but he couldn't quite fathom what.

Elya let his whole weight fall against the wall. He was overcome with a surprisingly forceful—yet clearly insane— desire to rush out to Ambit, grab his severed arm and lead him back to Core to get repaired. Only an equally strong desire not to relive the helpless rage he'd felt facing Kristoph in the hangar kept him magnetized to the spot.

Hedgebot had gone full red now, a color brighter and more dangerous than Imperial crimson. He had curled up into a tight knot. Shelled in like that, there was no way it would be able to come back to Elya on its own, at least not until he figured out how to control it properly. Did the bot need some sort of remote? Could he connect it to his tab?

The dull-knife smirk turned in Elya's direction, noticing

the glowing red hedgehog, and then catching a glimpse of Elya himself.

Elya whipped his body backward, but he knew it was too late. He thought about bolting, but he couldn't bear to let them take Hedgebot. Elya would die inside if they did to his bot what they had just done to do to poor Ambit.

Easy, little brother. Arn's voice came to him unbidden. Elya was still terrified, but the mental voice of his brother steeled him just enough to face what he had to do.

Elya darted out, scooped up Hedgebot in his hands, and sprinted all the way back to their little cabin at the north point of the station.

He'd never run so fast in his life.

FOUR

From the moment he ran scared from Kristoph like a dog with his tail between his legs, Elya fought an internal war with himself. On the one side was a potent desire to return to Core's shop, to learn more about bots and starfighter pilots—how to care for the former and whether it was possible for a humble farm boy from Yuzosix who collected bot parts to become the latter. Core's kindness and insight had opened a new galaxy of possibilities for Elya. At a time when the universe seemed intent on shattering any coherent vision of his own future, Core had given him a dose of hope.

On the other side was a blood-chilling cocktail of fear and shame. Fear for his safety, and shame for running scared. Core wouldn't have run scared from Kristoph, and neither would Captain Ruidiaz or even his brother Arn. Elya had been beaten up by bullies before, but something about the way Kristoph and his friends had laughed while Ambit was picking up his arm and trying to figure out what had gone wrong frightened him more than your average gang of bullies with three-to-one odds would have.

So, although he explored other parts of the station with Arn, over the next several days Elya steadfastly steered clear of the area near the hangar.

And then suddenly the Nevers were informed that it was time to depart.

"Already?" Elya asked.

"Finally," Rojer said, as if his younger sibling hadn't spoken. "I thought we'd be stuck here forever."

"It was less time than we spent on the Mammoth," Elya pointed out as he pulled on his rucksack and cinched the straps tight. Hedgebot ran along his shoulders and disappeared below the flap into the rucksack. The little dude loved walking all over Elya's arms and shoulders, and hiding in the pack. In just a few short days, the pokey metal claws had become as familiar a sensation to Elya as his nails against his own skin.

Rojer stared daggers at Elya, who cast his eyes downward reflexively and then was immediately mad that Rojer still seemed to have that power over him. He forced himself to lift his chin and meet his brother's eyes.

"Shut up," Rojer said.

"Make me," Elya retorted.

"Hush, both of you," Mom said. "Keep packing."

Elya did as he was told and after a minute so did Rojer, complaining the whole while. Except for Hedgebot, they hadn't acquired many things during their stay on Solaran's Bridge, so it only took a few minutes. Together, the Nevers clan made their way back toward the hangar. The closer they got, the more Elya fidgeted. Pretending his hands were infinite steps, he guided the restless hedgehog in an endless circular climb.

"Please, stop," Mom said, "you're making me dizzy, and I need you to pay attention to where you're going."

Elya did as he was told, though it took an effort of will

power to still his hands. He missed the comforting weight of the golden gear in his pocket. If he couldn't play with Hedge-bot, he had nothing to fidget with.

Near the hangar, their forward motion stalled as they came up against a crowd in the main corridor. They waited for the crowd to clear, shuffling forward with the rest of the refugees who had been cleared to leave today. Knowing they were in the east wing of the star-shaped space station, near the hangar, Elya's heart pitter-pattered in his chest.

"Remember, stick together," Mom said. She looked each of the boys in the eye, and they nodded their acknowledgment in turn. Her eyes lingered on Elya, and he felt his cheeks heat up. But this time she didn't say it. She didn't have to.

Don't wander off.

That thought combined with the crowded hallway triggered a memory, one he'd instinctually buried. Elya's palms began to sweat as his heart picked up speed. Suddenly, he was back on Yuzosix, at the spaceport where all residents had been told to go to evacuate the planet. There was one in the city near their home, but in the crowded rush of everyone trying to get there from hundreds of miles in *every* direction, it had taken them a full day and a half to reach the spaceport. By the time they arrived, Elya was exhausted, and the terminal itself had been overflowing with people. His mother had tried to be polite, had tried to wait their turn, but it was pure chaos and they had been forced to push their way onto the shuttle or risk being left behind.

"Stick together!" Mom had yelled over the raucous din as she pressed into the crowd.

Despite his best efforts, Elya got separated from his family. He had looked up just as Rojer disappeared ahead of him, and Arn, usually bringing up the rear, had somehow gotten in front of Elya without noticing he'd passed his brother. All of a sudden Elya was alone, practically invisible and underfoot in the crowd. Someone shoved him, he tripped and—

Arn touched his shoulder, causing Elya to jump and turn, squeezing Hedgebot to his chest.

"Easy, little brother," he said.

Elya sucked air through his nostrils, which seemed constricted and tight, like he was breathing through coffee straws. He closed his eyes, opening his mouth to gulp air, and forced himself to relax. The crowd was thick here, but this was the space station, not the spaceport terminal on Yuzosix. He was safe. He was safe.

Guided by Arn's gentle hands on his shoulders, Elya moved ahead slowly. Eventually they passed through a threshold into the hangar, and the crowd dissipated, or at least spread out into the larger space.

People were scattered everywhere, just as they had been on the day of their arrival, only this time, lines formed at the airlock entrances rather than the door into the station. None of the airlocks had been opened yet, though, nor did the Nevers know which one they were supposed to use. Elya's mother found an empty spot of floor and swung her pack down.

"I'm going to find out which ship we've been assigned to," she said as she rubbed her shoulders. "And grab a few supplies. You all wait here."

"Can I go with you?" Elya asked.

"No, honey, I'll just be a minute."

"Take him with you, then," Elya said holding out his bot. It was glowing blue now, but if she ran into danger, it would warn her better than anything else. "He'll keep you safe."

"Thanks sweetie, but I'll be fine."

She turned and vanished into the crowd.

Rojer rolled his eyes at Elya, pulled his tab out of his

pack, and began to watch videos to pass the time, slyly picking his nose when he thought no one was looking (they were).

Elya set Hedgebot down and watched it roam, the blue light glowing beneath its belly and lighting the grated floor of the hangar as it darted back and forth, scouting, seeking, searching.

"Hey little fella," a girl said, bending over to stroke Hedgebot's back. It was the blond from Core's shop, the one Arn had a crush on. In the time since meeting her, Elya had learned her name was Norah. "How are you getting along with our favorite little danger detector?"

Arn straightened next to him and shared a genuine smile with Norah. While Elya had avoided the area around the hangar in recent days, Arn had not, taking advantage of every opportunity he wasn't tasked with watching after Elya to sneak off and visit with his new girlfriend.

"He's great," Elya said honestly. "I just wish I knew how to get him to come back to me after he finds something that scares him."

"Oh, that's not too hard," Norah said, putting a finger to her mouth. "Hm, let's see...come stand over here for me." Elya did as she suggested. Norah waited while Hedgebot came around, then set a foot gently down on top of it, putting her weight gently down until it started to squirm. The light below it didn't change from blue, but it immediately curled up into a knot of metal.

"If it encounters danger for you, it turns red. If it runs into danger for itself, it generally curls into a ball. If either of these things happen, a simple snap of your fingers or a whistle will bring it back to you. Assuming it's not stuck."

Elya tried snapping. His first attempt barely made any sound, but on his second attempt he managed to make a bit of a pop. At the same time, Norah let up her foot. Hedgebot uncurled, scampered over to Elya, and crawled up until it sat on his shoulder.

"Wow, cool! Thanks."

"Sure thing. Mind if I borrow your brother for a second?"

Elya nodded. Norah took Arn by the hand and dragged him away. Elya rolled his eyes behind their back, but Arn only had eyes for the girl and didn't notice his youngest brother's contempt.

Unfortunately, that left Elya alone with Rojer, who he had no desire to spend any time with. He'd suffered enough of Rojer's badgering in front of the others and knew that it would be worse alone. Elya immediately set Hedgebot back down and moved a few yards away from his brother.

"Mom said wait here."

"What?" Elya said. "I can't hear you over the sound of you picking your nose." Rojer grimaced, mumbled something under his breath, and turned his back on his brother as he went back to watching videos.

This gave Elya the perfect opportunity to gain a healthy distance from his brother. He was careful to keep one eye on Rojer, and the other on Arn and Norah, who had ducked into a shadowy corner and were now making out and murmuring sweet nothings in each other's ears. Arn looked up once and caught his little brother's eye, and Elya immediately turned away as he felt his face heat up. When he first realized Arn's relationship with this girl had become serious, Elya had only felt annoyance and disgust. She was taking his brother away from him, after all. Now, for the first time, he felt it for what it truly was… jealousy.

Distracted by these strange and foreign feelings, Elya lost sight of Hedgebot. He found the blue light in the threshold of a doorway that led to the honeycomb of shops hugging the large hangar in a crescent-moon embrace. Butterflies flapped in his stomach at the idea of disobeying his mother, of sneaking away again, out of Arn's line of sight. But there were a lot of people out there, shopping. He would be safe in the crowd, wouldn't he? And with his reliable little danger detector at his side, what could go wrong?

Elya followed the tiny bot, who scampered into the hive of shops as he approached, always staying ten or twenty meters ahead of him, by design. Elya knew that he could turn around and go back to rejoin Rojer at any point, and that Hedgebot would follow him. But he chose not to. It felt good to face his fears. Scary, but good. He began to rehearse a conversation with Core in his head. The Chop Shop had been just around the corner to the left, hadn't it?

His mental rehearsal was interrupted when he caught sight of Hedgebot's blue light reflecting off a shiny object sitting in a hole in the airy, curved wall. He walked toward it, wiping his sweaty palms on his pants and trying to keep hold of the reigns on his excitement. It was a bot part, he saw as he approached, and one he'd never had in his possession before: a finger with two joints. The metal shell had a bluish tint that he'd only seen once or twice—a rare color. Elya took the lone digit and dropped it into his pocket, looking around to be sure no one had noticed him taking it. Streams of people walked by in the hall, each of them busy with their own objectives, bearing armfuls of bags and supplies for their upcoming journeys.

Hedgebot's blue light drifted forward. Elya noticed another metal digit in another hole in the wall further down the hall. He could have sworn he'd looked at that empty hole just a minute ago, but as the crowd passed he looked again and saw the metallic shine. Another finger. When he picked this one up, Hedgebot seemed to catch on to what he was doing. Elya found four fingers in the space of a few minutes, and was distracted thinking that perhaps Core would have a hand on which to mount them, when he reached the end of the shopping area.

He'd been so distracted by imagining the construction of his bot hand that he didn't notice he'd come to the end of the hall. There were no stairs at this end, but there were a few empty shops, gated by vertical garage-like doors that pulled down from above. Hedgebot went still, but its light stayed blue, indicating to Elya that there was no danger here.

Why, then, had the muscles in his neck and shoulders gone all tense?

"I knew he'd fall for the bait," someone said from behind him. "So predictable."

Turning around, Elya's stomach sank into his feet as he looked into a familiar dull-knife smirk.

One of the two bullies that had been with Kristoph when they ripped off Ambit's arm moved in behind him and lifted the sliding garage door that led to one of the empty shops. Kristoph and the other bully stepped forward, forcing Elya inside. His blood went cold, and the warring emotions of fear and shame flooded through his body. He fought to stay calm, but his heart hammered rapidly, his palms sweated, and his breathing became shallow.

Ambit stood inside the empty shop with his arms at his sides and his chin slumped onto his concave golden chest. The arm that had been torn off had been reattached—poorly. It hung down at a weird angle that made Elya certain it hadn't been done by Core or any kind of professional. The other arm ended at the wrist in a clump of frayed wires. No hand at all. The servant bot was on power-saving mode. Elya didn't know how they'd gotten the key to this empty shop, but he figured that Kristoph's merchant father had some weight with the shopkeeper's union, or maybe Kristoph and his friends had broken in. It didn't matter. Elya was trapped here with them, a thought that was cemented when they let the door fall closed, then flipped on some dim lights. If Elya ran for freedom now, that would only encourage them, make the punishment come faster. So he stood his ground. Hedgebot swirled around his feet. His light was still blue, but warming toward orange. No outright danger detected—at least not yet. The bot was useful, but for this kind of threat, it was clear that Elya's senses were more evolved.

"Did you get so bored torturing your poor bot that you have to pick on *me* now?" Elya demanded in a voice that quivered in the air of the empty shop.

"We were just having a little fun," Kristoph said. "Ambit can't feel anything. Isn't that right, Ambit?"

Ambit powered up and lifted his head to regard Kristoph with unlit eyes. "Yes, Master Kristoph," Ambit said. "I am a bot and do not experience physical pain."

What had they done to the poor bot? His defeated posture was like a knife to Elya's heart. And the missing hand…

Elya took his own hand out of his pocket, where he'd been unconsciously clutching the bot digits for comfort. Looking down, he noticed that his palm and fingers were wet and blue, as if he'd touched a freshly painted wall. He pulled out one of the bot digits and saw that the color had come off where his sweaty hands had been nervously rubbing the knuckle in his pocket. Beneath the fresh coat of blue paint, the original gold shone dully through.

Disgusted with his own gullibility, Elya removed all four metal fingers and tossed them at Ambit's feet with a mumbled, "Sorry."

Ambit bent down and gathered the fingers in his remaining hand, then stood and powered off again. Every bit the obedient machine.

"Sorry?" Kristoph scowled. "The only thing you have to be sorry for is how you embarrassed me in front of my father."

As he stepped into the nimbus of warming orange light cast by Hedgebot, Elya noticed that there was a deep reddish-purple bruise around Kristoph's left eye. Several smaller bruises mottled his upper arms, and Elya had the distinct impression, though he couldn't prove it, that the bruises had been caused by his father's angry hands.

Whatever pity Elya felt for the older boy was immediately trampled by a deep-seated sense of injustice that came bubbling forth, forming words before he could think to filter them.

Unable to help himself, Elya shouted, "You stole the gear from me! If you were embarrassed, you brought it on yourself."

Hedgebot's warning glow flashed from orange to fireball red, sending Elya's senses into overdrive. Time seemed to slow down. He reacted on instinct, leaning backward as something sharp and metallic sliced toward him in an arc.

If it wasn't for the split-second warning from Hedgebot, Elya never would have made it out of that room alive. But he did get the advantage of the warning, which is why the blade of Kristoph's pocket knife grazed his cheek instead of opening his throat.

He barely felt the cut. The knife's edge slid across his right cheekbone as he stepped backward and tripped over the boot of one of the other bullies, a heavy-set kid with curly hair and a condescending sneer that followed him to the floor. Elya landed and rolled and kept rolling, having learned from wrestling with his brothers that if you get a chance to gain some distance from your attackers, you better take it. He came up in a kneeling position, one knee on the ground, the other leg supporting his weight, facing Kristoph and bracing for a rush attack. That's how Rojer would have played it.

But Kristoph was far more cunning than his brother. Elya

panted hard, his heart pounding in his ears. He braced for an attack—none came. Instead, Kristoph leaned his weight on Hedgebot, who was stuck under one oiled leather boot.

"This is a neat little bot," Kristoph purred. "Where'd you get him?"

"He's mine! You let him go right now."

"Or what? You'll bleed on me?" He chuckled along with the other boys. The heavyset bully to Kristoph's right—the one that had tripped Elya—bent down and twisted one of Hedgebot's metallic claws, trying to pry it off. The hedgehog quickly curled into its defensive ball position. The other kid, a boy of Arn's age with long blond hair and a gaunt, underfed face circled slowly around, trying to get an angle on him.

Elya eyeballed the other boys as he raised a hand to the cut on his cheek, wiping away the wetness he felt there. Blood mixed with the blue paint in his palm, merging into a deep purple smudge in the dim light of the empty shop. He was still panting hard and scared stiff, but this time Elya refused to run. He wouldn't—he couldn't—leave his bot to suffer at the hands of Kristoph the way Ambit had. Bots couldn't die, and according to Ambit they didn't feel pain the way people did… but that hardly seemed to matter. Core had placed Hedgebot into Elya's care. Whatever happened to it was his responsibility now.

With a nod from Kristoph, the two bullies lumbered forward and began to pummel Elya with their fists. Their blows rained down like the worst hail storms on Yuzosix, and he had no shelter under which to hide. Elya tried to fight back, but he was too small and they were too strong. It took all his strength merely to keep his arms up to protect his face. They took advantage of every opening to bruise his ribs, kick him in the shins and beat him into the ground until he was curled into a ball like his bot.

Every time he tried to get up, they'd trip him and shove

him down again. There were only two of them, but it reminded him so much of his flight from Yuzosix, of getting lost in the maddened crowd, that the feeling of powerlessness he'd felt then came rushing back. Tears wet his face even as they continued to beat him.

When they finally got bored of kicking him, the thin bully and the heavyset one lifted him beneath his armpits and dragged him over to where Kristoph was shoving his pocketknife into Hedgebot's protective ball in an attempt to pry it open. This lit a fire in Elya. Despite the throbbing pain that filled his body, the sight of Kristoph torturing his bot renewed his determination. He vowed not to let them see how afraid he was.

"Make him open," Kristoph demanded.

Elya lifted his tear-streaked face and spit a mouthful of blood at Kristoph. It felt *good* to watch the older boy's face contort with fury.

"That's it! You're going to watch while I grind him into stardust!"

Elya thrashed in their grip, but the bullies held him tight. He was forced to watch while Kristoph smashed the heel of his boot down on Hedgebot over and over and over again. Still, this didn't seem to cause any harm to the bot—it was a sturdy little machine, built to endure danger and harm. Seeing that his efforts were ineffective, Kristoph tried his knife again, and when that didn't work, he found a heavy metal cabinet shoved in the corner of the office and made Ambit drag it over to him with his one good hand. The cabinet screeched as it scraped across the metal floor. And then Kristoph shoved it over and slammed it down on Hedgebot until its outer shell cracked.

"Hah!" Kristoph shouted in triumph, bending down and picking up his pocket knife once more. In a flash, Elya knew how they'd removed Ambit's hand and cut the frayed wires in his arm. Elya struggled harder in the grip of the two bullies. He could hear the breath of the heavyset one coming hard and fast in his left ear. They were getting tired from giving the beating and their sweaty hands were beginning to slip on his arms.

Elya leaned as far forward as he could, angling down toward Hedgebot. The bullies hands slipped down to his wrists. He lunged backward and thrust his body upward, bashing his head into the fat bully's double chin. The older boy cried out and released Elya's arm. He didn't look to see what kind of damage he'd caused, but he would have bet that the warm wet droplets that splattered the back of his neck weren't water. He used the leverage he now had to twist around, causing the thin bully holding his other arm to cuss and scrabble for a better grip. Elya's knee in his groin finally caused him to release the hold on his wrist.

So intent was he on trying to shove his knife into Hedgebot's innards that Kristoph didn't immediately move to help his companions. But when Elya came after him, Kristoph finally turned, slashing his knife out at him again in anger. This time Elya anticipated it. He hopped backward and the knife caught in his shirt, entangling the two of them and momentarily capturing the little pocket knife. Elya felt the cold blade against his skin and twisted, trying to get away from the sharp edge and failing. He was stuck. Kristoph sneered and seethed, spittle bubbling between his clenched teeth and spraying into Elya's face. But Elya was just as angry now as Kristoph was. No one attacked his bot and got away with it.

He grabbed the hand Kristoph used to hold the knife and forced it away from his own chest. They struggled like this, pushing and pulling each other until Kristoph got his feet tangled in the legs of the thin bully, who was still groaning and clutching his groin on the ground.

When Elya felt Kristoph stumble, he shoved outward and released his hold on Kristoph's knife-hand. Expecting resistance from Elya and finding none, Kristoph fell backward, windmilling his arms and throwing the pocketknife across the room. His hip slammed against the metal cabinet he'd used to crack Hedgebot's protective shell. He used his hands, now empty, to brace himself against the cabinet—and suddenly began to seize.

Elya inhaled sharply through his nose and felt his eyes go wide. He and the two bullies watched, jaws gaping, as Kristoph shook with powerful tremors. Smoke began to rise from where his palms met the metal cabinet. Terrified and confused, Elya gathered his wits and sprinted to the side of the room, where the pocket knife had landed. He picked up the knife, turned—and that's when he finally understood what was happening.

Kristoph shook like he was having a seizure, his whole body rocking back and forth. His hands were stuck to the cabinet as if they'd been glued there. The frayed wires in Ambit's severed wrist were touching the side of the cabinet, infusing it with electrical energy. That energy flowed from Ambit's power source, through the cabinet, and into Kristoph through his hands, electrocuting him.

Sparks lit the room when Ambit finally removed the frayed wires trailing out of his wrist from the metal side of the cabinet. His eyes lit up. The bot turned his head toward Elya and nodded, almost imperceptibly. Then his chin fell to his chest as the light faded from his eyes, and he powered off completely, his power cells depleted.

Kristoph slumped and fell to the ground with a thud. He didn't move.

Bearing the knife in front of him toward the two bullies—who, while not unconscious like Kristoph, were still dangerous—Elya stepped over to Kristoph's side. The bullies watched him but didn't interfere. Whether they were afraid of Ambit, now, or afraid of the knife he held, Elya neither knew nor cared.

Using his free hand, he carefully collected Hedgebot. The red light went cold and faded to a pale blue at his touch. He set the bot aside, then, gathering his courage, Elya reached into Kristoph's tunic and felt around. He sighed in relief when his hands came into contact with a familiar set of finely cut teeth. Elya removed the golden gear that Kristoph had stolen, and stowed it carefully in his own pocket.

Picking up Hedgebot in one hand, and bearing the pocket knife in the other, Elya backed slowly out of the room, keeping the other boys in his sight until he bumped into the door. Kristoph remained unconscious with smoke curling in the air above him. The other two clutched their wounds. Crouching on trembling legs, Elya hauled the door up with his knife hand and slipped away.

FIVE

Wrung out and ragged, bruised and beaten, Elya stumbled into Rojer and Arn, who had been running madly around the hangar and through the shops, frantically searching for him.

They shouted with joy when he collapsed into their arms—even Rojer seemed happy to see his little brother—and then demanded to know what had happened.

Elya didn't want to talk about it. He cradled Hedgebot and cried silently. But when his mother came back and saw the state Elya was in, with his cut cheek and bruised body and battered bot, she absolutely lost it. Elya was forced to explain what happened just to get her to calm down and stop raging in front of everyone. An audience of gawking people had gathered, and all Elya wanted at that moment was to get out of their sight.

Instead of calming his mother down, his story seemed to enrage her. She dragged Elya in front of a pair of security guards and demanded that Kristoph and the other boys be taken into custody and charged with assault.

Elya didn't object. They deserved it. But he was too tired

to show much enthusiasm. Elya led the guards to the empty shop. Neither Kristoph nor the other boys were to be found. But the blood-spattered evidence was all over the floor, and Ambit was still there, handless and unresponsive next to the cabinet, standing with his head lolling forward and no sign of life in his eyes.

If servant bots weren't built to look like people, perhaps it wouldn't have affected Elya so deeply. As it was, the depressing sight of the tortured bot sent him spiraling. He retreated to a corner and sank to the ground with his back to the wall. "He's gone catatonic!" one of the guards said when Elya failed to respond to a string of inane questions.

Adults could be real idiots sometimes.

"I already told you what happened!" Elya said. "Can't you see? Just leave me alone."

"I think that's quite enough," Mom said, stepping in front of Elya and forcing the guards to give him some space. That his mother defended him and didn't heap blame on him for wandering off—though, of course, he did—was the kindest thing she had ever done. Elya had never loved and admired her more than in that moment. Nor had he ever felt so guilty for disobeying her.

An investigative unit was called in. After a few hours, Kristoph and his confederates were located. Kristoph had woken up and stumbled back to his parents' cabin, where his father had been hiding the boy, and lying to the investigators. The other two were discovered cowering together in a storage room.

The investigator told his mother that the boys would be punished, which seemed to satisfy her. She let them know she'd be checking to make sure Kristoph's father didn't find some way to get the Imperial Inquisitor to lessen their sentences, or conveniently "dismiss" the case.

"It's in the Empire's hands now, ma'am," the investigator replied.

When it was all over, Elya was relieved to learn that the whole ordeal had caused Kristoph to be placed on a different Mammoth longhauler. They were forced to stay behind for an Inquisitor to project in on the Ansible network and pass their sentence, while the Nevers were allowed to go.

"Please, can I take Hedgebot to Core to get fixed? Please, Mom. I'm begging you."

Hedgebot beeped sadly in Elya's arms.

"We don't have time, hun. They've already delayed their departure for us. We'll get the bot fixed when we get to the settlement, I promise."

As luck would have it, word of what happened reached Core. Elya's heart soared when he saw the machinist and his blond assistant waiting for him at the mouth of the airlock. Core handed Elya a heavy bag. It had the tristar insignia of the Solaran Empire printed on both sides.

"That's a machinist's repair kit. I just transferred an instruction manual to your tab. You'll do fine if you just follow the instructions."

Norah and Arn embraced and whispered a tearful goodbye. Core looked at the two of them and smiled sadly.

"Will Hedgebot be okay?" Elya asked.

"Don't worry, kid," Core said, "Any damage to a bot can be repaired with the right parts and enough patience."

Elya took a deep, trembling breath and let it out. All of his fear and shame seemed to be expelled with it. He thanked Core, and then followed his brothers and mother through the airlock and onto the Mammoth that would take them to their new home.

<h1 style="text-align:center">SIX</h1>

Ever since they became refugees, Elya Nevers collected bot parts.

He didn't know when this habit had formed, or how the idea had first come to him. But it didn't matter. It was a part of him now. Elya Nevers collected bot parts. It was who he was.

And not just bot *parts*. Elya, who grew up poor on a rural solar farm and had never been able to afford a bot of his own, now had Hedgebot, a danger detector all his own. A bot who had saved his life.

It took him several weeks to repair Hedgebot. Fortunately, the trip to their new home took longer, so he had plenty of uninterrupted time to focus on the problem. He read the instruction manual from beginning to end, watched every video twice, and practiced on his bot and any other spare parts he could find until his fingers ached.

The many spare parts he'd been collecting came in handy. Using a small welder and other tools he found in the repair kit Core gave him, along with the parts he had collected and a few more he scrounged together on the new Mammoth, Elya was able to restore the bot's broken outer shell.

"I'm proud of you," Mom said as she watched the bot scurry happily around the room, curling into a ball and uncurling several times as he tested his newly repaired defensive function. "You worked hard on that."

"Pretty incredible, little brother," Arn said.

They all turned to Rojer. "Yeah, it's all right, I guess."

Elya burst out laughing and threw his arms around Rojer. "I love you, brother. Even if you are a grump."

Rojer groaned. "Are we there yet?"

Elya craned his head around and stared off through a porthole into the black expanse of space, mottled with stars. He spotted a giant orange marble in the distance, around which several settler's moons were said to orbit. "Actually, it looks like we are."

Elya snapped his fingers and Hedgebot scurried up his leg and perched on his shoulder. The Nevers family crowded around the porthole and watched as they drifted closer to their new home.

RAPTOR

BOOK 2

ONE

Casey sat alone in the conservatory among her mother's overgrown menagerie of exotic plants and fought against a tightness in her chest.

The funeral had taken place nearly two weeks ago. Hundreds of well-wishers had come and gone, but the tightness never left. A hard knot lodged behind her sternum that ached when she breathed, especially when she thought about Mom—a brilliant, beautiful, nurturing woman who had been taken from these worlds too soon.

"Miss Osprey," said a robotic voice, startling her, "your father would like to see you in his study."

Casey glanced through a tangled knot of green, blue and purple foliage to where XB-9, their family's servant bot, stood just inside the doorway to the conservatory. Casey hadn't heard the motion-activated glass doors slide open. She'd been lost in thought, drifting through memories, drowning in grief.

That happened a lot lately. She'd run out of tears, but the sadness came unexpectedly and at the most inopportune moments. Like right now, looking at XB-9 through the veil of her mother's beloved plants. Leafy vines spilled over the edges of their containers. No one had trimmed them back in months. After Mom fell ill, only the room's automated watering system kept them alive. A thick beard of tangled moss tumbled down to brush against the chromed top of XB-9's bucket-shaped head.

Casey sighed and turned back to look at the flowers in front of her. Across from the bench seat, a Torch Lily was in full bloom. These flowers were among Mom's favorites. A dozen brilliant, brush-like heads the color of the sun faded to twilight at their base.

"They bloom in waves as the season fades from summer to autumn," Mom once told Casey as she, maybe six or seven years old at the time, stared raptly up at the tall blonde goddess. The conservatory was Casey's favorite room in the house—because it was her mother's favorite. She made Mom bring her here every morning and every evening, and would ask her to name each flower. She hardly remembered all their names now, but she remembered the way the light made a halo out of Mom's long hair. She'd loved watching her talk about things she loved more than Casey had ever loved anything herself. Anything except her mother.

"These flowers are the bridge between the seasons. Their blossoms have to be pruned as they fade so they don't steal water from the ones trying to bloom next."

In Mom's final weeks, Casey had tried her best to follow those instructions. Her mother hadn't been strong enough to get out of bed, let alone care for her plants. The ones that needed constant care had already faded, shriveled and died. But though she clipped the withered gray flowers of the Torch Lily with the same clippers her mother used, something had gone wrong. The new flowers coming in now were weak and pale, dying before they even had a chance to blossom.

So much potential for beauty, withered by the shadow of death.

"Miss Casey?"

She sighed. "What is it, bot?"

"Your father requests your presence, please."

Casey's gut churned as XB-9's message finally penetrated the fog and registered in her mind. Why didn't he just come down here himself?

But, of course, she knew why. Dad hadn't entered the conservatory since Mom got sick. This was her mother's space—Dad had no interest in flowers or plants. No interest in anything except the Fleet and the endless Kryl War. In the early days of Mom's diagnosis, he'd still been running around the galaxy on various missions. She didn't think she'd ever forgive him for that. He called it his "duty." But wasn't a father's duty to his family first? It seemed so clear and obvious to her. She didn't understand what was so important that he kept getting pulled away.

"His heart is in the right place," her mother once told her. This was near the end. Her voice had become thin and raspy. She had trouble holding her head up off the pillow for more than a few minutes at a time. "Don't hold a grudge, okay? He's doing the best he can."

"Miss Casey," the bot interrupted again, a threatening optimism edging his voice into a higher pitch, "would you like me to carry you upstairs on my shoulders?"

"I'm not a kid anymore, Niner." She used to love riding XB-9's shoulders around the family manor's many rooms and sprawling grounds (sprawling for Ariadne, at least. Casey had been ten when she first developed a sense for how rare property ownership was on the Solaran Empire's capital planet). He had been her personal steed. Her ever-present companion. Also—she had realized as she entered her teenage years—her bodyguard.

"Technically, your are a minor until your sixteenth birth—"

"I'm thirteen."

"You are twelve years and nine months old."

"Close enough."

His speakerbox flashed, indicating humor. "Close only counts in horseshoes and hand grenades," he said in a tone of voice more pleasant than she could muster.

Casey had added Old Earth idioms to XB-9's language database a couple years ago. Mom loved them, and Casey had taken a shine to them, too, even though she had never seen a horse *or* a hand grenade in real life. The thought pulled a dark veil over the cradle of life and color in which she sat.

Casey decided she couldn't stand the conservatory any longer. It had been like that for the past few days. Her heart would ache for her mother, so she'd walk across the house and sit here, but after a little while, it made her too heartsick to stay put. Movement usually helped. She jumped to her feet and strode past XB-9, timing the breezeway's automatic doors so that her shoulders brushed their edges as she passed through.

"What's Admiral Grump want this time?" she asked XB-9, who trailed behind her.

"That's *Inquisitor* Grump now, Miss Osprey. He has accepted the promotion. The Emperor himself pinned on his new rank."

Casey's foot caught on a fold of the carpet that lined the hall, and she stumbled. "Figures. Is that why he wants to see me? To tell me about his new job?"

"He told you he was going to take the job over dinner last night."

"Oh." She didn't remember that. "Are you sure?"

"Quite certain, Miss Osprey. A servant bot's recall is

47.5% more reliable than a human being's, and 99.997% accurate according to manufacturer tests."

"Whatever."

She reluctantly trudged up the curving staircase, through the library, and into her father's office.

"Casey," he said, or rather, he sighed, almost like she'd been lost and suddenly found. "There you are."

She narrowed her eyes and gazed suspiciously up at her father. He was a handsome man with the noble bearing of their ancestors—broad shoulders, chiseled chin, and a head full of onyx hair whose color was the exact opposite of hers and her mother's. He still wore his military dress uniform from the day's work, navy blue with crimson piping running down his shoulders, arms, and legs. The only concession he'd made to comfort was unfastening the top buttons of the coat and letting the large lapels hang open, partially obscuring the growing rack of medals mounted on his chest.

His face was shadowed by a multi-day growth of salt-and-pepper beard, and there were deep creases at the corners of his eyes, whose lids were bruised-looking at the bottom.

It was the first time in her life she ever looked at her father and thought, *He's not as young as he used to be*. Months of her mother's home hospice care had aged them both in unexpected ways.

Casey said nothing, just waited as a small troupe of dancing creatures lurched around inside her nervous stomach.

"You ah... have you and XB-9 been having fun?" He winced as the words fell flat over the surface of his giant mahogany desk.

"Not really." She glanced sidelong at her childhood playmate. XB-9 was a bot, and she'd always have a soft spot in her heart for the big metal idiot, but fun? Come on. She wasn't a kid anymore.

"I see."

She couldn't remember the last time her father had tried to have a real conversation with her. She'd long grown weary of his war stories and pithy sayings about duty, honor and planet. She'd never be a soldier like him, and she grew tired of being speechified to. Casey's vision shifted behind her dad to more medals hanging in shadow boxes on the wall, to his drill sword from the Fleet academy mounted horizontally above them, and to the many models of battlemechs and starfighters projected as holovids onto the walls around the room. He loved the Fleet. He *was* the Fleet—or at least a cog in its vast machinery, their newest justice of the peace. Inquisitor Osprey: If any soldier in the Solaran Defense Forces broke a law or disobeyed orders, they'd have to face her father's wrath.

She didn't envy those unfortunate souls. She looked everywhere in the room but up at Dad. The dancing troupe in her belly did another somersault.

Inquisitor Grump took a deep, steadying breath. "My new job is going to keep me very busy."

She stared at him, saying nothing.

"I'm going to be traveling quite a lot. I won't be able to control my schedule like I used to."

"I'll be fine. XB-9 can keep me company. The cooks already know what I like to eat."

"You're still a kid, Casey."

"I am not! I'm almost thirteen."

"Almost." He smirked at her.

"I'm practically an adult," she insisted.

Her father's smile turned into a grimace, or a rictus, or whatever it means when you smile and your head looks like a bare skull.

The dancing troupe dropped out of a trap door in her gut.

She knew that face.

Her father was about to become what her mother would have called "intractable."

"I know you are," he said. "But what if there's an emergency? What if something serious happens while I'm gone?"

"I've got XB-9."

"Even with his latest firmware updates, he's still not human, and you know how I feel about that."

Casey's breath came fast. She wiped sweaty palms on her pants. "Mrs. Jordan is right next door. I can always ask her for help."

"And if she's not home? Or if she is and she's started drinking earlier than usual?"

"I don't know! You've got plenty of money. Why don't you just hire someone to watch the house?"

He took a deep breath and settled into the antigrav chair behind his desk. It sank as his weight fell onto it, and then levitated up an inch or two. "I've been talking to people I trust at work, people who have been in my situation before, and they've given me a new perspective."

"What are you saying?"

"It's not just about emergencies, Case, or about the house. I need to know you're well cared for, otherwise I won't be able to focus on my work."

"Why is it always about you? What about what I want?"

He nodded. "I've thought a lot about that."

"Well, you never *asked me*, did you?"

He winced. "I know you'd rather stay here, sweetheart. The memory of your mother is all around us, and we both miss her like hell."

Tears sprang to her eyes. This was the first time since Mom's funeral that Dad had acknowledged, out loud, how much he actually missed her. Casey's vision went blurry and she couldn't see her father's face.

Only the way his voice thickened told her that he, too, was holding back tears. "You need more than I can give you. Especially now, and more than ever once I begin my new job as an Imperial Inquisitor."

"So don't take the job!"

He bowed his head. "I have to, Casey. It's my duty."

"No you don't! You always say that! Your duty should be to your family. To me and Mom!" She still couldn't bring herself, in this horrible moment, to admit that she was gone.

"It is, sweetheart."

"Don't call me that! You're a liar. You don't even care about me!" Tears were openly streaming down her face now. Her hands had tightened into balls and she realized she was screaming at her father. She couldn't stop herself.

"I do, Casey. More than you can imagine. Which is why I got in touch with the headmaster at Polar Prep—"

"No," she said. "No, Dad, please."

"—and managed to secure a spot for you. The school year has already begun, so you'll have to do a little catch-up on your coursework, but you'll have all the support you need there. You'll make friends and have great teachers and—"

His words shook her to the core. "I don't want to go!"

"—and I'll know you're somewhere safe, with people who can watch over you."

Tears ran down her cheeks and the tightness in her chest clawed up to her throat, where it choked out a scream. "YOU DON'T KNOW THAT! Something could happen! Even at school I could get sick like Mom, and—and then what? Who will be there for *me*?"

Her father rushed around the desk and wrapped his arms around her before she could escape. She banged her fists against his chest, against his thick shoulder muscles. She struck him and thrashed in his arms. He said nothing, just let her rail against him and wipe her tears on the undershirt inside his open coat. She struggled against him with all her strength, until she couldn't any more. Resistance left her suddenly and when she collapsed, he knelt on the floor and held her tight.

"I love you, Casey. I wouldn't do this if I had another choice."

"You do! You *always* have another choice."

He bowed his head and sighed wearily. "It's not that simple."

"You always have a choice," she insisted. "You taught me that."

"I know it doesn't seem like it, but I promise this is the best option of the choices available. Polar Prep is where I went to school. I think you'll like it there, once you get used to it."

She sniffed. "I already hate it."

He chuckled. "You haven't even seen it yet."

"I don't care. I miss Mom."

"Me, too, kiddo. Me too."

TWO

A frozen wind cut through Casey's synthweave parka. Steps unfolded from the ornithopter and she descended to the rocky, windblown tundra.

She glared at the bleak landscape as the roaring of the vehicle's many blades died down. Dry snow swirled around the feet of her father and XB-9, who had descended first and were now looking back at her, waiting patiently.

Her father squinted into the icy wind. He wore a thick cap with earflaps, and had donned an overcoat over top of his sharply pressed Fleet uniform. XB-9 was unaffected by the biting cold apart from a little stiffness in its normally oiled movements. The servant bot held her suitcase in one metal hand and her backpack in the other. All her belongings packed into two little bags. Her whole world.

She'd only been allowed to bring along two other small concessions to personality. One was a potted plant from her mother's conservatory—a miniature tree-like shrub called a ficacia. She held it safely next to her body beneath her jacket. Casey had consulted the cyclopedia about the plant's needs and the north pole's weather patterns, and had been reassured that if it was kept inside, in a spot with enough sunlight, the miniature tree would be able to survive the cold climate.

The other object was the holovid of an osprey her mother kept on her bureau in her room. The small disc fit in her palm and projected a life-like facsimile of the extinct bird from Old Earth after which her family was named. It was the only bird Casey had ever seen, since avian species didn't exist on Ariadne (although they populated some of the settler's moons). Mom, having adopted the Osprey family name after they got married, had a fondness for the ancient hawks. The moving image projected by the holovid showed the predator diving into a wide river and coming up with a fish gripped in its sharp talons.

In order to face life at Polar Prep, Casey would need to be just like the raptor—a solitary predator, afraid of nothing.

Even though she felt more like the fish than the bird right now.

"Let's go, Case," her father said. "Don't want to be late for your first day."

Fear nothing, she told herself. *You're an Osprey.*

She gulped and was glad the sound was masked by the roar of the biting wind.

They began to trudge uphill. The cold quickly numbed her cheeks and fingers, even through her mittens. She held onto the potted plant inside her coat with one hand, while the other gripped the flat disc containing the holovid in her jacket pocket.

As they crested the hillock, Casey got her first glance at Polar Prep's campus. A sprawling structure made of 3D-printed stone, it was designed to look like a modern castle, complete with turrets and ramparts and a vast gate. She'd seen photos on the cyclopedia, and read that it was constructed this way because, in the early days of the Fleet's training, the tundra around the north pole was filled with large mammals which posed a potential danger to the kids.

Nowadays, the population of large mammals had been hunted to extinction, or forced onto the ice caps farther north to find better access to the highly valuable commodity of liquid water, which was so rare on Ariadne.

The Empire needed all the water it could find to sustain its population. The native species were left to fend for themselves.

She wondered what her mother, a xenobiologist, would have thought about that.

The castle loomed larger as they approached until it towered overhead. The landing pad was situated nearby and it took about fifteen minutes of walking to reach the gate. They passed sporting fields and standalone trailers and other outbuildings on the way.

As expected, the headmaster stood just inside the gate, hands in thick mittens, waiting for them.

"Welcome, Inquisitor! Miss Osprey. How was your trip?"

Or should she say, "headmistress?" Though she was bundled up in a thick parka of her own, there was no doubt based on the shape of her face and hips that this was a middle-aged woman. Due to her father's work, she was well aware that the Fleet liked to use "sir" for everyone, even female commanders—by way of tradition—but would the academy do that, too?

"Little bit of turbulence, but otherwise as expected," her father said.

"And what have you got hiding in that coat, dear?"

Casey's nose wrinkled at being called "dear," and at being called out on the ficacia, which she had hoped to smuggle in unseen. "A plant," Casey said.

"Very well, nothing against plants here—if you can keep them alive. And were you able to complete the checklist we sent ahead of time? Uniforms, school supplies and such?"

The woman's eyes seemed to have an uncanny ability to pierce through the thick parka straight into Casey's soul. "Yes."

"Good. I'm Ms. Pravada. We use the masculine form of formal address, Fleet fashion, so if you find my name challenging, you can also call me Headmaster, or sir." That answered that question. "Welcome to Polar Prep, the only Fleet Academy on Ariadne. You arrived at a good time. Winter is just about to set in."

"This isn't winter?" Casey blurted out.

"Oh, Animus, no, dear, this is a balmy autumn day where the sun is still shining. Now, come along, I'll give you the tour and then show you to your room so you can get settled in."

Her father gave her a smile that wasn't at all reassuring. Ms. Pravada turned, marched through the courtyard and led them into the school, pulling off her mittens as she went.

Casey had always thought the Osprey manor was big, which meant Polar Prep was enormous. They walked through a vast entryway decorated with school memorabilia and filled with trophy cases, down a long hall lined with lockers and classrooms, past an auditorium, two gymnasiums, chemistry labs, supply closets, and other rooms whose purpose she couldn't fathom.

At the back of the building, a set of curving stairs took them upward past groups of girls and boys who were younger than Casey, more who were her age, and others who were much older. Some of them wore navy-and-crimson uniforms, while others had on casual clothes. A group of girls passed, perspiring like they had just come back from a ten kilometer run. Casey couldn't figure out why nobody was in class until she remembered that it was Saturday.

At the second level, she had to unzip her parka because she'd begun to sweat, more from nerves than physical exertion or temperature. She took out the potted ficacia and inspected it. It had done all right, a little crinkled but none the worse for wear.

The second level of the school was much like what she'd seen on the first, but with more kids milling about. As they toured the building, Casey became self-conscious of her appearance. She wasn't dressed like the other kids. She also didn't know anyone here. They all seemed to be wandering around in little groups, and even though she didn't want to be at Polar Prep, she couldn't help but feel left out. Maybe for the first time in her life, she truly felt like an outsider.

They strolled through a library filled with comfy chairs set around low tables for studying. Holoscreen terminals lined many walls, and about half of them were occupied. At this point, she realized that Ms. Pravada was giving her father the full tour, and the two of them were in close conversation about how extensive Polar Prep's collection of holovids was, about their ratio of students to teachers, and about the military style drills and athletic teams they ran as extracurricular programs. Casey swallowed a nervous fear. She'd never played team sports before and, while it sounded like fun, she knew it meant that she would have to make friends and get along with other people.

Friends meant ties. And ties meant that she would really be stuck here.

She crept a bit closer to XB-9, taking comfort in his familiar metallic presence.

Upon exiting the library, they mounted another curving staircase. This one led up to a third floor. At this point, she suspected that they were at the top floor of the school.

Instead of classrooms, this floor seemed to be lined with dormitories and offices.

They stopped for a moment in Ms. Pravada's surprisingly large office where her father filled out a few forms on a holo-screen tab, and asked the headmaster a lot of questions about tuition, holidays, visiting regulations, and school curriculum. Had that much changed since he'd attended the academy? Maybe he just wanted to be sure.

Casey lost interest and her mind wandered. After a few minutes she got bored of hearing them talk, and her restless feet carried her out into the hallway.

A group of older girls—women, really, whose shapely bodies made her self-conscious of her own stick-thin form— sat in a ring of armchairs beside a floor-to-ceiling window at the end of the hall. It looked out behind the school over a snow-dusted meadow that climbed up to a single imposing mountain in the distance.

At first, she mistook the women for teachers themselves. But they couldn't be teachers, they were still too young, and at least a couple had on the uniforms of the school.

One of them, a raven-haired beauty with stunning cheekbones and perfect skin sitting in the center of the group, jerked her chin in Casey's direction and put her hand over her mouth to mutter something to the others. They all erupted in giggles and snickers and turned to look at her, then laughed even harder.

Casey realized that XB-9 was hovering behind her, still holding her backpack in one hand and her suitcase in the other. Her face heated as she heard the phrase "nanny bot" drift down the hall.

Her face burning, Casey turned away from the pretty girls to find that her father and Ms. Pravada were just coming out of the office.

"Now, are you ready, dear?" Ms. Pravada asked, "I'll show you to your room, and give you some time to get situated."

Ms. Pravada led them past the clique of older girls, who continued to snicker and whisper as they went by. One of them received a sharp look from Ms. Pravada, but the headmaster did nothing to intervene, although Casey felt certain that it would have been different had her father not been there.

She didn't think it was possible, but Ms. Pravada opened the door on yet another staircase. As they went up this time, the hall seemed to narrow and the ceiling slanted downward. There were dorm rooms here, each with a number and a card reader beside it. Ms. Pravada swiped a card at one about halfway down the hall, and the door swung open to reveal a bare single room.

A twin bed was pushed up against one wall, a shelving unit on the other, and a desk—more like a table, really—was mounted beneath the window opposite the door. The ceiling here slanted down to meet the top of the window and gave the dorm a cramped feeling. XB-9 had to bend double just to walk inside. The bot set her suitcase and backpack down on the bed before returning to the hall to stand watch.

"Heck of a view," Dad said, pointing out the window, which looked upon that same cold, lonely mountain. "What do you think, Case?"

"I hate it," she said, honestly.

Ms. Pravada frowned at her. Casey averted her eyes.

"I don't want to be here, Dad. Why can't I just go with you?"

Ms. Pravada smiled tightly and left the room.

"I already told you Casey," Dad said when they were alone. "I can't take you with me. My work is demanding and often dangerous. And they don't allow minors on Imperial destroyers anyway. You'll be safe here. You'll make friends. And you'll learn a whole lot—things I'll never be able to teach you."

"That's not true," she said, and couldn't keep the whining tone out of her voice. "I could… carry your sword, or take notes, or remember things. I have a good memory. You told me that yourself."

"You do, Case. The best. But what I need you to do now is be here. The best thing you can do for me is study hard and make friends. Be a teenage girl again. Live your life. That's what I need you to do. I need you to live a normal life."

"This isn't normal!"

"You don't think all those other kids are living normal lives here?"

"I don't care," she said. "It's not fair!"

"Little of life is." Her father gently pried the ficacia from her grip. She hadn't realized she had been holding it with such force. Her fingers ached as she let go and she slowly made fists, her cold fingers cracking as they worked out stiffness in the knuckles and tendons. Her skin was already dry from the cold.

He set the plant on the desk in a beam of light slanting in through the window.

Yearning for a sense of rightness, Casey pulled out the holovid disc and set it next to the ficacia. Flicking it on, the osprey appeared, ruffled its feathers and began to preen itself. Her father knelt and hugged her hard. She thought she heard him sniffle. When they separated, his eyes were rimmed with red, but he forced a smile anyway. He had that look on his face again, the intractable one, and with a sinking feeling in her gut she knew there would be no changing his mind.

"I'll see you soon," he said, "They allow visitors during the fall break, and then you'll come home and spend winter break with me. Write me every day if you want to. Send me videos over the ansible. I'll respond as soon as I get your messages, no matter where in the galaxy I am."

She didn't trust her voice anymore, so Casey just nodded.

"I love you, Casey."

"I love you, too, Dad," she cried, flinging herself back into his arms.

Eventually he extricated himself and walked out into the hallway.

"Farewell, Miss Osprey," said XB-9 in his normal tone of cheer. The bot pivoted on one foot and followed her father. Casey walked out into the hall after them, blinking back tears that made the walls seem to wave and press inward, and the angled ceiling to sag down on top of her.

Snickers sounded behind her, and Casey heard that phrase again.

"Nanny bot… must be some rich girl."

"Inquisitor's daughter," another kid said.

"Bet she doesn't have any real friends."

Casey's ears burned. She tried to blink back the tears, but they escaped and rolled down her cheek in embarrassing rivulets.

What would her mother think of her standing here in the hallway and crying as her daddy left her? With a spark of defiance, Casey threw back her shoulders so she stood proud like Mom had taught her. She made it safely into her room and managed to close and lock the door before the sobs overwhelmed her, wracking her chest with great gulping hiccups.

Casey didn't remember crying like that before. Not when her Mom died, not at the funeral, not ever.

She'd never felt so alone.

When her tears were spent and her nose was red and raw Casey stood, and went to the ficacia by the window.

A leaf had fallen off. It was resting on the desk and had already started to turn brown around the stem.

She vowed not to be like the dead leaf. Not to give up. Even though her father had abandoned her, she wasn't about to let Mom down.

<h1 style="text-align:center">THREE</h1>

Ms. Pravada had been right. When Casey arrived at Polar Prep, Winter hadn't even begun to set in.

Over the course of the next month, temperatures plummeted, the biting wind sharpened its teeth, and snow fell endlessly to cover the tundra.

It wasn't wet snow, like the kind that coated the lawn of the Ospreys' garden in a mushy carpet once or twice a year—if she was lucky. This snow was dry as bone dust and drifted into dunes like sand, reforming the topography around Polar Prep daily, obscuring the footprints and walking paths made by students as part of their exercise routine—which they bundled up for each morning in gloves and hats and layers upon layers of wicking synthweave underclothes.

When winter came to the northernmost livable region in Ariadne, it came swiftly and without mercy.

Casey spent the first month of school drifting from classroom to gym to auditorium in a reclusive fog. She was still so angry about being packed off to a boarding school—a military prep academy, of all places—that she hardly spoke for fear the acid of her resentment would spill out onto the people around her. It didn't help that most of the other boys and girls seemed happy here. They laughed a lot, and played games, and joked around. The teachers were strict—especially about uniforms and personal hygiene and homework—but not mean about it or drunk on their power the way some of the private tutors her father hired when she was younger had been. And all that made it worse because in her heart of hearts she *wanted* to hate this place. She was determined to pick out every facet of ugliness and magnify it to prove to her father that he'd been wrong, that leaving her here was a mistake. He may have been selected by the emperor for his ability to objectively pass judgment in matters of Fleet law, but in this matter his vision was clouded.

She'd prove it.

So it was with a kind of grim determination that Casey shuffled into her third period Solaran history class, seething with anger. She picked a desk in the back corner where she could draw ospreys on her tab, and the near-sighted Mr. Hobbs wouldn't call on her too often.

She had the outline of a round head on the screen and was working on getting the shape of the beak right when the kid seated next to her leaned over and said, "What's that, some kind of flying xeno?"

"What?" she said, taken aback by such an accusation. "No, of course not, don't be stupid."

Maybe it was because she'd slept fitfully last night, or maybe it was because she was worried about her ficacia tree dying. It had dropped a dozen more leaves since she'd arrived and was now close to looking like the skeleton of a winter Solstice tree. Whatever the reason, she immediately felt guilty when the kid jerked back and turned away.

"I'm sorry," she said, reaching out to put her hand on the kid's shoulder. "I shouldn't have snapped at you. That was mean."

It took Casey a minute to figure out that this thin, boyish figure was a girl. A girl with a terrible bowl-shaped haircut—the kind you get when your parents are too poor to send you to a hairdresser—but a girl nonetheless. Hairdressers had been thrilled to come to the Osprey manor when Casey or her mother needed a trim. Not even Dad did his own hair.

The contrast shocked some manners back into her. She thought her mother would be ashamed of her behavior and rushed to make up for it.

"I'm Casey," she said. "What's your name?"

The waif of a girl timidly peered out at her from under those uniform level bangs and whispered, "Alia."

"Pleased to meet you, Alia."

The look on the girl's face veered between pain and confusion. Had anyone *ever* said anything nice to this girl before? Did anyone even notice her? With a hot flash of guilt, Casey realized that she hadn't. They'd been in the same class for weeks together and this was the first time Casey had really seen her.

Under her hand, Casey could feel Alia's sweater was threadbare and worn. Her blue-and-crimson uniform skirt was patched multiple times. The patch jobs were good, but the way the pattern skipped a square of cloth was unmistakable.

Alia kept her silence, so Casey answered her original question in an effort to get some conversation going. "It's not a xeno, by the way. Maybe it looks like one because I'm not so good at drawing, but it's an osprey, a fishing hawk from Old Earth."

"I've never seen a bird before..."

"Ospreys weren't the biggest birds, not by a longshot, but they were fast, and tough, and they could dive bomb into the water from hundreds of feet in the air, spear a fish in their talons, and climb back into the sky faster than you could blink." Her words came out all in a rush. This was the first time since she'd arrived that Casey had been excited about anything, and she felt a little embarrassed to show it; embarrassed but exhilarated.

"Why an osprey?"

It took Casey a moment to realize she was asking why Casey chose to draw this creature, of all things. "It's my family mascot. Osprey's my family name. Casey Osprey."

Alia's eyes widened into twin holodiscs. "You're the Inquisitor's daughter. I heard about you. Thought you'd be older... didn't realize we'd be in the same class together."

Casey snorted. "I *wish* I was older. If I was, I'd emancipate myself and get out of here faster than you can say Kryl meat."

Alia frowned, and then shrugged. "I'm glad I'm not. I like it here. It's better than being at home..."

Her voice trailed off as Mr. Hobbs strode into the classroom and clapped his hands, bringing the room to attention. "Settle down, people, settle down," said Mr. Hobbs. "Eyes to the front, please. We have a special guest today."

He was followed by the tall, buxom brunette Casey had seen on her first day—the one who seemed to be the ringleader of the group of girls who made fun of her "nanny bot."

She was stunningly beautiful. Long curvy legs, high cheekbones, an artful amount of makeup expertly applied to bring out the rose tones in her brown skin. Her eyes were a deep green and she gazed around the room with perfect, superior calm. Her uniform was pressed and new—not like the threadbare skirt Alia wore—and her sneakers were spotless white.

"This is Renata Spector, a senior at Polar Prep and candidate for Class Captain."

"Mr. Hobbs!" Renata said, "The election hasn't even started yet."

"I know, dear, but no one will be surprised when you win."

She batted her eyes at him in a way that made Casey feel *very* uncomfortable. She squirmed in her seat and deepened the lines of the osprey's wings on her tab. The proportions were just… off. A poor facsimile of the holovid in her room. She snapped her pen down in disgust.

"Ms. Osprey, is there something you wish to share with the rest of us?"

When she looked up, the whole class had pivoted in their seats to stare at her. She cleared her throat. Had she made some kind of noise? She hadn't meant to.

"No, sir," she said in the smallest voice she could muster. Alia pulled her cheeks back in a *don't wanna be ya* sort of grimace.

"Very well." Mr. Hobbs turned back to the stunning young woman beside him. "Renata, the floor is yours."

"Hello, everybody. I'm Renata Spector, and Mr. Hobbs asked me to come here today because I grew up on Oltanis, the Empire's fifth colony. He wanted me to share with you what it was like, and a little about our culture. The first thing to know is that unlike Ariadne, Oltanis has *lots* of water, mostly salt-water, with little landmasses covered in thick jungle. I grew up on the main island…"

Renata spoke about her homeworld for about fifteen minutes while Mr. Hobbs cycled the holoprojector through images of a thick jungle, a foggy swamp, and a small city made out of the recycled skeleton of a Colonial Voyager. The boys in the class hung on every word while their eyes traveled along Renata's shapely curves, and whispered undoubtedly lewd comments to each other.

The girls didn't seem physically attracted to Renata—well, most of them didn't—but they too listened with rapt attention. If the boys wanted to sleep with her, the girls wanted to *be* her. Even Casey found herself getting drawn into Renata's aura, idolizing her and wishing she could be more like her—older, more attractive, more confident, more popular… if Polar Prep Fleet Academy had a queen appointed by the divine right of Animus, it would be Renata Spector.

For her part, Renata drank in the admiration of her younger counterparts. She obviously had some experience playing to the crowd. Whereas Casey, were she up in front of the class, would have collapsed in on herself in a fit of nervous anxiety, Renata absorbed their attention and seemed to transform it into energy. Like a Torch Lily basking in a golden ray of the late-summer sun.

When she finished her speech and departed, headed back to wherever it was seniors went for the second half of third period, the air seemed to chill at her passing. Energy drained from the room and her classmates shook themselves as if waking from a dream.

Chief among them, Mr. Hobbs. "Well, then, uh, where were we, where were we…? Ah, yes! Please open your tabs to the chapter on the founding of the Solaran Empire's first colony…"

After class, Casey wandered out of the room, still thinking about Renata and the possibilities she represented. Could Casey find her place among the student body like the older girl? Not that Casey ever thought she'd be so popular, or have cheekbones fit for a holovid actress… but might she find a place here to grow into herself? To figure out the person she wanted to be? It was an interesting question, and for the first time since she arrived at Polar Prep, she actually considered that it might not be so bad as she had first assumed.

Casey had just opened her locker and deposited her tab when she spotted Alia to her left, down the hall, talking to a couple of dark-haired older girls. Casey recognized them as being on the fringes of the clique that constantly surrounded Renata, jockeying for her favor. Not the most popular, but definitely part of the in-crowd.

Alia hung her head so her bangs concealed her face, and clutched her tab to her chest in a defense posture as she tried to lean back out of the conversation. But the lockers were behind her, and with the girls on either side, there wasn't anywhere for her to go.

"What's this?" asked one of the girls as she fingered the patch job on Alia's skirt. Alia tried to shove her skirt back down, but the older girl had the fabric firmly in her grip. She smacked Alia's hand away and bent down to examine the fabric more closely.

As she did, the skirt rose up, revealing Alia's stick-thin and pasty legs… marked with criss-crossing, raised red lines at the tops of her thighs.

"Pretty shoddy work, kid," said the girl. She had on so much makeup Casey could see a definitive line beneath her chin separating the orange-colored cake from her natural skin, even from this distance. "Did you sew this yourself?"

The other kids laughed. A group of boys from their Solaran history class snickered and bent down to get a good look at Alia's panties.

"Stop it," Casey said. The words were out of her mouth before she'd thought about what she was saying.

She was ignored, her voice smothered in the laughter of dozens of students. A fury rose up in her like none she'd experienced since her father told her she'd be packed off to Polar Prep. Casey slammed the locker door and marched in their direction.

"I said, stop."

Again, they didn't even glance in her direction. The girl with too much makeup on was running her fingers forcefully through Alia's hair, and then rubbing her fingers together and examining them like they'd been dipped in a vat of oil. Alia squirmed and tried to run away, but the other girls shoved her back each time she tried.

Beyond the pair of bullies, Renata leaned against a doorway and chatted with a couple of handsome boys who looked like they played on the velcross team. She was facing Alia, so Casey *knew* she could see what was happening.

And yet she did nothing.

"Stellis, Mandi, please, just let me *go*," Alia whined to the older girls.

Her begging only made it worse. Stellis and Mandi—she thought Mandi was the one with the makeup problem, while Stellis was long-limbed and had big hands—threw their heads back and laughed.

"Awww, poor baby," Stellis crooned.

"Go on, cry for your Mummy now," Mandi said. "You always do."

Alia's lower lip began to quiver as she fought back tears.

"I mean it makes sense, she is such a baby," said Stellis. "Look at that chest. I've had bug bites that are bigger."

Alia's eyes caught Casey watching and seemed to shrink in on herself even further. Casey glanced over at Renata again, hoping she would intervene. Renata had influence with these girls—Stellis and Mandi looked up to her. If Renata told them to stop, she wouldn't be ignored.

But Renata just laughed at some dumb thing the boys were saying, and made no move to intervene.

"Screw this," Casey muttered. Then, loud enough for her voice to cut through the laughter and chatter: "I said, stop it!"

Stellis slowly turned to face her. "Oh, new girl has a voice after all. Are you trying to give me orders? I don't see any Inquisitor's scales on *your* shoulders."

"Get your hands off her."

"Or what?" She peered melodramatically up and down the hall. "You'll sic your nanny bot on me?"

"Or I'll make you."

Mandi and Stellis both threw their heads back and cackled.

"Suuure you will." Mandi stepped close, still chuckling, and leaned her head down so Casey could see the line of makeup and how it had begun to run with perspiration. "I'll give you one warning, rich girl. You better turn around and walk away or you'll regret it. You don't have your nanny bot to protect you anymore."

Casey made balls of her fists and shook with rage—and with fear. She'd never been so terrified. Mandi was only about half a foot taller than her, but the fact that she was an upperclassmen, she had friends here, and that *no one* had said a word while they were tormenting Alia showed clearly which direction the power flowed in this school.

And Renata Spector just watched it all happen.

Casey's only advantage was the element of surprise. She reached up, twined her fingers into Mandi's hair, and yanked down *hard*.

Mandi squealed like a broken servomotor and clawed at her face with one hand while she reached up with the other to try to break Casey's grip. Stellis jumped on her, and together they shoved Casey to the ground, kicking her hard in the stomach and ribs.

Casey scratched and kicked and fought with all her strength. A hand struck her in the face. She grabbed it and bit down hard, drawing the taste of metallic blood.

Someone yanked her back. It was over as fast as it had started. The whole altercation had lasted the space of a few heartbeats.

"That's quite enough of *that*," said Mr. Hobbs, who was gripping her shirt in both hands. Two other teachers were hauling Stellis and Mandi to their feet. Casey didn't realize she'd managed to take both of them down. A fierce pride filled her. She spat blood on the floor and grinned at the older girls.

Alia, for her part, seemed to have escaped. Casey peered up and down the hall. The little waif was nowhere to be seen.

Would her mother be proud of her for intervening? *Yeah, she would have been.* The thought boosted her spirits.

"Let's go," Mr. Hobbs said, "Upstairs, to Ms. Pravada's office. Now. March."

FOUR

Ms. Pravada frowned at Casey through a pair of half-moon spectacles that rested on the tip of her long nose. Her dark eyes were focused on a middle distance only visible to her.

It wasn't just Casey she saw, but her entire academic history in the heads-up display projected through those lenses—inscrutable and infinite, like the workings of the ansible that connected the colony worlds and the Fleet's warships.

"You've only been here a month," Ms. Pravada finally said, "and yet the list of complaints from your teachers and your classmates is longer than many students who have been attending this institution for years."

Ms. Pravada read from the list, extending a finger with each item like she was reciting the sins of man from the Book of Animus. "She doesn't pay attention in class. She doesn't socialize with the other students. She eats nothing but cookies and bread. She puts the bare minimum of effort into her physical training. She skates by on her natural intelligence." Ms. Pravada arched a single plucked eyebrow. Whoever submitted *that* piece of feedback, Casey didn't think it was Mr. Hobbs, who believed her duller than a basic bot and half as interesting.

"And now, to top it all off, you're picking fights in the halls. By Earth, girl, what has gotten into you? Do you *want* to be punished?"

Casey gripped her lips firmly together and said nothing. The answer was a fervent *Yes*. Moreover, she dearly hoped her punishment consisted of expulsion and a first-class ticket back home to the Osprey manor. She didn't dare speak such a thing aloud, however, for fear she might jinx her chances.

Ms. Pravada plucked the glasses, shining with the faint blue lights of the administrator's HUD, off her nose, and set them on the desktop. The chair she sat in wasn't like her father's expensive hoverchair, but one of the old-fashioned kind with wheels that squawked as the headmaster tilted back. "I know you don't wish to be here, that much was clear from the start. But the least you could do is make the best of the situation. Your father is paying good money for your education, young lady, and you're repaying him by making every attempt to squander it."

That wasn't fair at all, but Ms. Pravada was at least correct about how she felt.

Whether she wanted to be here or not, Casey wasn't going to apologize for fighting back against injustice wherever she found it. Her mother had taught her to stand up for equity and fairness. Even when it got her into trouble.

The thought of her mother brought the pang of memory back, which caused an ache in her ribs that smarted when she breathed in. Although, that was probably the spot where Stellis had kicked her more than the memory of her mother. Already, her muscles had begun to bruise yellow-green. She'd checked under her shirt while she waited to be called into the headmaster's office.

"Well?" Ms. Pravada said. "Aren't you even going to attempt to defend your actions?"

"Didn't you hear the story from Stellis and Mandi? And Mr. Hobbs, and the other teachers?"

"Yes, of course I did. You saw them all parade in here. And now I will hear your version."

That was only fair, wasn't it? She had thought Ms. Pravada many things, but fair hadn't sprung to mind as a primary descriptor. That surprised Casey. If Ms. Pravada judged the situation fairly, Casey would definitely *not* get sent home for fighting.

Well, crap. She heaved a sigh. "Ow," Casey muttered, clutching her ribs.

Another arched brow angled down at her from across the desk.

"Fine. It's pretty simple, really. Stellis and Mandi had Alia trapped against the lockers. They were picking on her, grabbing at her skirt and showing all the boys her panties. Running their fingers through her hair. Teasing her and crooning insults. I told them to stop. They didn't listen." She shrugged. "So I made them listen."

"You certainly made one thing: Enemies. Maybe now instead of picking on Alia, they'll torment you."

"So, what, I should have stood by and watched while they bullied Alia? That's not right."

"You should have gone and gotten a teacher, who would have taken care of it without causing an altercation that resulted in more of my students getting injured."

Casey crossed her arms and looked out the window, where fat snowflakes drifted through a strangely windless afternoon. *Yeah, right,* she wanted to say. By the time she went and got a teacher, Stellis and Mandi would have switched tactics, or dispersed, or played dumb, or made up some other excuse. By that point, it would have been too late to intervene and help Alia. She told Ms. Pravada as much.

"I don't agree with your assessment. All the teachers have de-escalation training. You do not. Next time this happens, you are not to get involved. Fetch an adult—a teacher, me, I don't care who—and we will deal with the situation properly, according to our policies. Understood?"

She wondered if her father would agree with that. Casey crossed her arms and returned to the comfort of her silence.

"Am I clear? I need to hear you say it."

"Yes, Ms. Pravada," she said reluctantly.

"Good. Now, as to your punishment..."

Her heart skipped a beat. She leaned forward in her chair.

"... you've earned thirty hours of community service."

Her beating heart sank into her stomach. Not being sent home after all. *Earth, blast it.*

"You'll spend an hour a day for the next month cleaning dirty classrooms and common rooms, in the evenings during your free time and on weekends at sunrise. Mr. Hobbs will give you your assignments. You will keep track of the work you do on your tab, and submit a video summary to me at the end of each week."

A nervous anxiety clawed at her throat. "What about Stellis and Mandi? Do they get the same punishment?"

"Not that it's any of your business, but no. They have their own community service to perform."

That was a relief. She didn't ever want to be caught alone with them. A tendency toward forgiveness didn't seem like one of their personal traits.

Ms. Pravada interlaced her fingers on the desk and watched Casey with a carefully schooled expression.

"You believe me, don't you?" Casey asked. "I was just trying to help Alia."

"And trying to get sent home all at once. How convenient that you could pick a fight in an attempt to get your way. You'll find that I am not a pushover, however, and it will take an awful lot for me to expel you. We are used to disobedient students here. You are not the first, and you won't be the last. Now, you're to report to Mr. Hobbs tomorrow night at sixteen hundred hours sharp. And remember, if you want to help a friend, there are better ways than fighting with upper-class students."

With that, she was dismissed. Casey managed to attend math and biology, her last two periods, and then trudged slowly up to her dorm room to nurse her bruises and change into sweatpants. She'd found a few rips in her school uniform she hadn't noticed before, and was wondering if she should attempt a home repair, like Alia, or if she had enough credit left this month to order a replacement outfit.

Alia was waiting for her, sitting on the floor with her knees hugged tight to her chest. As Casey approached, she stood and brushed herself off, then darted her eyes warily up and down the hall.

"You want to come inside?" Casey asked.

Alia nodded rapidly several times.

She swiped the door open. Once they were inside, she checked to make sure it was firmly locked behind them.

Alia stared at her ficacia tree for a moment—which had dropped another four Earth-cursed leaves onto the desktop —before turning back to Casey.

"I wanted to say thank you… for standing up to Stellis and Mandi earlier today."

Casey, who had been in the doldrums since her scolding by the headmaster, felt her chest swell with pride. "You're welcome. They're jerks, you know."

Alia bobbed her head. "They think I'm an easy target."

"You shouldn't let them intimidate you." Casey thought about what Ms. Pravada said. "Have you ever tried to tell a teacher about them bullying you?"

"It would just get worse, if I did. Not to mention make me look even weaker."

Casey twisted her lips. She wasn't wrong. "We'll think of something."

Alia's expression grew guarded. "We?"

"Yeah. I'm not going to leave you alone to deal with those bullies."

Alia's face transformed like a flower in bloom as a smile formed dimples in her cheeks.

"Here, let me show you what an osprey *really* looks like." Casey stepped over to the window and activated the holovid with a touch. The majestic hawk soared over the ficacia, its wings spread to their fullest length, before diving down into the water and flapping back up with a fish.

Alia's gasp and squeal of delight brought joy to her heart. Like a tree starved for water, washed by a summer rainstorm.

After that, Casey and Alia cleaved to each other like earth and sky. While, at first, Alia's obvious adoration made her uncomfortable, they quickly grew familiar in each other's company and the awkwardness passed.

They didn't share every class, and Casey couldn't watch over Alia every single minute of every day to ward off her tormentors. Instead, she did something better. She tried to imbue Alia with the innate beliefs of confidence and self-worth Casey's mother had taught her. It wasn't an overnight change, but over the coming days and weeks, Casey could see how each compliment, each piece of praise added some steel to her spine, how each discussion caused Alia to stand up straighter. For her birthday, which was just two weeks after they met, Casey bought Alia a trip to the school hairdresser —a bot stylist, not a person. Still, the tapered pixie cut she ended up with complemented her facial structure much better than the boyish bowl cut she'd worn before. Casey had also ordered sparkly nail polish that was delivered to her window by a drone, and they spent the evening giving each other manicures and talking about boys they liked.

In the meantime, Casey tried to do her community service with the kind of patience and grace her mother would have mustered. Cleaning graffiti off desks and scouring pots in the kitchen was far from glamorous work, but she found she liked the feeling of accomplishing something, of setting right, of making the world a little bit cleaner and straighter than she found it. Her dry hands blistered and bled being in and out of the water and cleaning chemicals all the time, but even that held its own fascination.

Mr. Hobbs was hard on her at first, pointing out when she was a single minute late or when she missed a dust bunny under a desk, but once she knew how he liked things —especially his own classroom—he stopped being so demanding and let her come and go as she pleased. After the elections for class captain began, he barely even noticed when she walked into the room. His star pupil, Renata, was running for the position, of course, and Casey found the two of them plotting Renata's campaign together in the evenings on more than one occasion.

She kept her distance when Renata was there. Not that it was hard. Teacher and teacher's pet hardly deigned to glance in her direction.

Casey's favorite part of the whole experience of community service, though, was getting acquainted with the secret ways of the back of the house—the people and passages that made Polar Prep run like a smoothly oiled machine: the laundry facilities which always emanated a warm scent of spring and steam; the chefs who showed up before dawn on Saturday mornings to prepare the hot pancake breakfast that was the school favorite; the teachers' lounges with their late-night aleacc games; the janitors' supply closets overflowing with cleaning chemicals and mops and buckets; and the halls that connected all of them, weaving behind the classrooms and offices, siphoning auditorium speakers through gymnasiums and locker rooms, taking sick students from the nurse's office to their dormitories without encountering a single person.

Casey loved to explore these hidden ways. They, more than anything she'd yet discovered at Polar Prep, reminded her of home. The Osprey manor, too, had its winding passageways where the maids and servant bots went from dining room to library, and she loved walking them. This familiarity with the back of the house responsible for Polar Prep's smooth operations gave Casey a new appreciation for the people (not to mention the bots) who ran the school, and a feeling of gratitude towards them she'd never felt before. No longer did she take her hot meals or clean clothes for granted.

She was walking through one of these hidden ways, bringing her cleaning supplies back to the storage closet when she stumbled into another one of Ms. Pravada's "situations."

The closet was adjacent to a chemistry lab, and the easiest way to get there was to cross through Mr. Hobbs' classroom. Casey was walking along, bopping to some electronic music piping into her headphones, when she stepped through the back entrance only to look up and find herself face to face with the lower half of Mandi's chin.

The orange line of makeup on her neck wasn't so obvious today, but her glossed lips were pinched and wrinkled. Behind her, Stellis stood up from a computer terminal, the holoscreen of which displayed a table of rankings and names. Renata was manipulating a set of numbers, carefully dialing them up and down.

Casey's eyes reflexively scanned the data, noticing the names of other students she recognized… And then Mr. Hobbs' pudgy face in the top right of the hologram, showing that his account was attached to the sign in.

And then she remembered that today was the last day to vote for Class Captain.

Ms. Pravada's advice about getting an adult rang sharply in her mind, and Casey turned, cleaning supplies in hand, to retreat the way she'd come, anxiously trying to wipe what she'd seen from her mind.

A hand reached out and snatched at her shirt. She was jerked back, and the bottles and rags in her arms went tumbling to the floor.

A bottle of bleach water burst and began to dribble out onto the cold tile. Stellis leapt out of her chair and grabbed Casey's left arm. Mandi took the right, and together they dragged her back out of the puddle and pinned her down.

She cried out, and began to struggle, but Renata was on top of her suddenly, straddling her chest and shoving a dirty rag, balled up, into her mouth. Casey gagged on the taste of bleach.

"Shut up, you stupid bitch," Stellis hissed.

Casey halted a scream while it was still in her throat.

"I thought you said the door was locked!" Renata whispered to the other two while she held one hand down over the rag in Casey's mouth. The pressure on her throat was too much and her breathing was labored as she struggled under their weight.

"It was," Mandi said. "She came in through the back hall from the teacher's lounge."

"What was she doing in the teacher's lounge?" Renata demanded.

"Earth, I don't know, Renata."

Renata gritted her teeth and released a slow breath. "Fine. It doesn't matter now." Her eyebrows knitted together as something caught her eye. Renata retrieved a shiny object from the floor, and came back to sit on Casey's chest, flipping the flat disc of Casey's mom's holovid in her hand.

"What's this?" she asked in a taunting voice.

Renata set it down by Casey's head and activated the holovid. The shimmering hawk circled majestically overhead, its wings spread wide.

Even though she was on her back, the bottom of Casey's stomach dropped out. She liked to bring the holovid with her on her nightly round of chores. It kept her company. She hadn't even noticed that it had fallen out of her pocket when they yanked her to the ground.

Renata flipped the disc over. Her father had inscribed her mother's name on the metallic base plate there when he gave it to her as an anniversary present.

"Oh, *that's* right," Renata said. "You're the girl with the dead mom."

Casey bucked wildly against her captors' restraints. They were all twice her size, though, and with the two girls holding her arms and Renata sitting on her chest, she couldn't escape.

"Listen to me, little bird," Renata said. And Casey really did feel like a little bird—pinned to the floor by these catty women, a fragile little creature with her wings clipped. Stellis shifted her weight so she knelt on Casey's wrist. The sharp pain that shot up her forearm made her whimper involuntarily.

"You didn't see anything here tonight, okay?" Renata said. "If I find out you spoke a word of this to anyone, I will make your life so miserable you'll beg your daddy to come rescue you. Do you hear me?"

Tears began to leak out of her eyes. Against her wishes, Casey nodded her understanding. Anything to end this torment.

"Good," Renata said. "Because if you say anything, if I even hear you drop a *hint* about this—even to your little friend with the bad patch job—you'll be a *dead* little bird. Do we understand each other?"

Again, she nodded.

Renata pulled the rag out of her mouth. Casey gasped a few ragged breaths in. A chemical taste coated her tongue and cheeks.

"I want to hear you say it."

Renata must have had an encounter or two with Ms. Pravada. Still, Casey knew when she was beat. "I do, I swear. I swear!"

"I'm keeping this as collateral." Renata switched off the holovid and palmed the disc. "To make sure you behave."

"No!" Casey said, but Renata twisted away and pocketed the device.

Renata nodded at her cronies. Stellis and Mandi picked their weight up off Casey's shoulders and wrists. She rolled over to her hands and knees and panted, dry heaving twice. Thankfully, nothing came up except the awful chemical taste.

"Hey, little bird," Renata added. "Clean up this Earth-damned mess you made. No one can know you were here."

And so Casey was made to clean up the spilled bleach water while her three tormentors looked on, pointing out the spots she missed. By the time she was done and had finally returned the cleaning supplies to their closet, her spirit was a raw wound that had been scored with nails.

She retreated to the safety of her room and lay awake late into the night. When she finally did fall asleep, she kept startling awake at every creak of the building, while the winter wind howled outside her window.

FIVE

asey stood over her bare-limbed ficacia tree, rotated her sore wrist, and stared out at the snow-covered foothills.

It was full winter now, and the forecast gave every indication that there would be *months* of this kind of weather to come. She'd hated it when she got here. Now, it suited her mood: bleak, cold, harsh.

Barren.

"You *have* tell Ms. Pravada," Alia said. "They can't get away with this!"

"They already have," Casey said. "It's too late."

"If you say something, the headmaster can reverse the decision. She'll see the truth. She always does."

"Will she? Is that why you went to her with your problems when *you* were the one they were bullying?"

That was a low blow, but Casey was tired of arguing. She turned in time to see Alia's face flush red. Alia knew instinctively the same thing Casey did—that if Renata was caught in the act, something could be done about it. But if you whined about it to the teachers days later, you were just another tattletale.

No one likes a tattletale. No one believes them, either.

"It's not right," Alia insisted. "They can't get away with it. She cheated to win!"

"You think I don't know that?"

Alia hadn't been like this before. A month ago, she would have hunkered inward and bottled up her anger at the injustice, keeping her eyes down and minding her own. Apparently, Casey's influence had made an impact. On any other day, she would have thought Alia's inkling of a spine was a positive outcome. But as much as she agreed with her, Casey didn't think going to Ms. Pravada now was the right strategy.

Not if she wanted to see her mother's holovid again.

"If I'd gone straight to Ms. Pravada the night I walked in on them in Mr. Hobbs' classroom, maybe she would have believed me. But it's been *days*. They already announced the election results. In everyone's mind, Renata's already class captain. If I say something now, it just looks like I'm jealous."

She hadn't even wanted to tell Alia, at first. But she had to tell *someone*.

"You're not! There's got to be a way to prove it. You said they were using Mr. Hobbs' tab. They can look at his history. Or… or… security footage, or something."

"I already checked about video footage. It's against Imperial law to record video of minors on school property. If they kept video of us, parents wouldn't send their kids to school here. As for Mr. Hobbs' tab…" She shook her head. "If that was going to get them caught, they never would have done it in the first place. Renata must have found some workaround in the system. They were logged in on his device, with his credentials, after all."

Alia flopped down on Casey's narrow bed and sighed. "It's just not right…"

"I know."

"So, what're you gonna *do*?" Alia asked again.

Casey had recorded several messages to send over the ansible to her father about the situation, but when she played them back it always sounded like she was whining. He was in another star system, working a case on Yuzosix, one of the more established colonies. Even if her father wanted to help her, he couldn't.

"I'll think of something," Casey said.

She ran her fingers along the brittle branches of the ficacia tree. It was still alive, but the cold and relentless cloud cover had been hard on it. She'd purchased a heater and a UV lamp to give it both a little more warmth and more light. But all the leaves had fallen off anyway, despite her best efforts. Clearly, she didn't have her mother's green thumb.

Casey went to class that morning disheartened, wondering what her mother would have done.

She would have taken matters into her own hands, surely… she would have demanded justice. But what did that mean in this situation?

If Casey went to Ms. Pravada like Alia wanted her to do, then Renata would hide—or worse, destroy—the holovid before it could be recovered. Assuming Ms. Pravada even believed her in the first place.

If she went at Renata herself, the same thing would happen. And probably worse.

It seemed like she was caught between a rock and a hard place.

Casey chuckled wryly. Those Old Earth idioms just wouldn't leave her alone.

She wished XB-9 were here. He could be her muscle. Not that he ever would have let Renata and the other girls attack her in the first place. But he wasn't here, so it didn't matter.

That was just wishful thinking. She was really on her own with this one. If she could just—

Casey was jolted out of her own thoughts and back into the present by the impact of her head with the metal door of a locker.

"What are you mumbling to yourself about, little bird?" Stellis crooned. She brushed out her hair with a tangled round brush and flicked the ends in Casey's face.

"None of your business," Casey said as she leaned away.

Mandi took a bottle of iced tea out of Casey's backpack, popped it open and took a big swig. She made a face as if it was gross—it wasn't, peach-flavored tea was Casey's favorite—and then spit her backwash into the container before replacing it in the mesh pocket on the side of Casey's pack.

"It is our business, little bird," she said. "We have to make sure you're planning on keeping to our agreement."

Casey glared at her.

"Well, are you?" Stellis asked.

"Of course," Casey said.

"Good," Mandi said. "Wouldn't want us to have to kill any birds, now, would you? They're already an endangered species."

Casey experienced several of these torment sessions over the following days. Renata would be standing in the hall outside her class before the bell rang, ostensibly waiting to talk to Mr. Hobbs or one of the other teachers, but really to spy on her. After gym class once, while she was showering, all her clothes disappeared from her locker. During an early morning training run, Stellis would fall back to motivate and coach up the laggards—of which Alia was always one—and "accidentally" trip Casey, then demand that Alia pick her up.

There were a thousand other slights. Eating off her plate at lunch, knocking her bag off her shoulder in the hallway, banging a fist on her door late at night and startling her out of a sound sleep. Stealing the laces out of the snow boots she left in front of an air vent to dry.

They never let up. Ms. Pravada had been right. Not the first time, when she initially came to Alia's defense, but Casey *had* made enemies of the girls.

After one particularly embarrassing situation involving ketchup stains on the back of her skirt during lunch, Casey fled through the back halls to the nurse's office filled with shame.

"What's the matter, hun?" the round-faced nurse asked. Mrs. Mora was a kind woman in her fifties, plump and motherly, stern but caring. All the kids loved her because she gave them a safe place to escape to when they needed space to breathe.

Casey clenched her jaw around the words she wanted to speak. She'd never had to run to the nurse's office before and it was galling that she'd ended up here. But she didn't know where else to go, and her feet took her here of their own accord.

"You can talk to me, you know," said Mrs. Mora. "This is a safe space."

Casey nodded. She was on the verge of giving up and just blurting it out. *RENATA RIGGED THE CLASS CAPTAIN ELECTION AND STOLE MY MOM'S HOLOVID.* Ugh. Even the idea of it disgusted her. She sounded like such a little baby.

"I can't," Casey said. But oh, how she wanted to…

"Whatever is bothering you, your secret is safe with me. I promise."

"If I don't tell you, nothing changes," Casey said, her voice hoarse and on the verge of tears. "If I do tell you, *she'll* find out and then I'll lose something dear to me."

"Sounds like a lose-lose situation."

"That's one way to put it."

"Let me help you. I have resources. You can trust me, sweetheart."

Mrs. Mora's face was so open and kind, so caring, that in this moment of shame-filled weakness, Casey decided, all of a sudden, to just let it out. "I caught Renata rigging the class captain election. She cheated so she could win, and she made me promise not to tell anyone, and then she took my mom's holovid and won't give it back."

By the time she was done speaking her face had crumpled in on itself and embarrassing tears were rolling down her cheeks.

Mrs. Mora blinked at her. Then she said, "Renata?"

Her tears dried up immediately at the shock of the nurse's disbelief. "That's what I said, isn't it?"

"It's—it's not that, child. It's just… are you sure it's Renata Spector you're talking about?"

"Yes, I'm sure! Of course I'm sure."

"And you say you caught her *rigging* the election?"

"Yes." A cold tingle crept down her back and shoulders. Casey straightened and wiped the tears from her cheeks. "You don't believe me."

"It's not that I don't believe you," the nurse rushed to say. "It's just a big accusation."

"Stellis and Mandi are pulling these pranks on me *because* they're afraid I'm going to tell on them."

"Have you told any of the teachers about this? Have you shared it with Ms. Pravada?"

"Well, no, because Renata has my mom's holovid. She stole it from me and is holding it hostage. And you *can't* tell them I said anything, or they'll destroy it or at least hide it, and then I'll *never* see it again."

"What's so important about that holovid?"

"It's the last thing I have of my mom's…"

"I see. I'm going to have to discuss this with the headmaster."

"No!" Casey said. "You said I could trust you. You can't tell her. Please. You can't."

"If what you're saying is true, then she needs to know."

"*If* what I'm saying is true? *IF?*"

"Well, dear, it's a serious accusation, and—something like that is grounds for suspension, at the very least. Maybe expulsion."

"Forget it. Forget I ever said anything." Casey pushed herself off the chair on which she'd been sitting and made to leave. Mrs. Mora stepped in front of the door, blocking the only way out.

"Now, listen, I didn't mean to panic you. But you have to understand that a serious accusation like this will require an investigation. And you say you haven't reported this to anyone else?"

"No," Casey said in a small voice that reminded her more of Alia than of herself. "I already told you that."

"I just… I don't understand why you'd wait this long to say something. Why didn't you report it when it first happened? It's been almost a week since the election ended."

Which is exactly what she'd told Alia would happen.

"I said, forget it," Casey said. "I'll deal with it myself."

Casey shoved past her back into the hall. She'd completely forgotten about the ketchup stains on her skirt, and the sounds of the other kids laughing behind her back in the lunchroom.

It should have been fifth period now, with all the kids in class, but as she hurried through the halls back to her locker to get her backpack before retreating to her dorm, there were a surprising number of people milling around in the hallway.

They barely saw her. She knew something was wrong

when the eyes of Stellis and Mandi slid over her without so much as a second glance.

Something had gone terribly wrong while she was in the nurse's office.

As Casey approached her locker, Alia saw her and came running.

"Alia, what's happened? Everyone is acting so strange."

Alia swallowed and worked her mouth a few times.

"Alia? Alia! Tell me. What happened? Was there an accident? Did somebody get hurt?"

Alia swallowed and then wet her dry lips with her tongue. "We just got word. The Kryl invaded Yuzosix. They had to evacuate the planet, but not everyone got out in time."

"Oh, Animus," Casey said. Her own shock at the news overrode her personal anguish and made her own problems seem small and insignificant.

And then chills crawled down her whole body. Her father was working a case on Yuzosix.

"They're estimating that eight million Solarans are dead," Alia said.

SIX

Casey sent message after message over the ansible, but there was no response from her father.

Six hours later, a knock came at her dorm room door. Casey met Alia's eyes over the hologram projected from her tab. They had been playing games to distract themselves from the news, and watching their cyclopedia feeds in the background for any sign of survivors.

None had yet been found.

Casey got up and cautiously cracked the door open.

"Come with me, please," said Nurse Mora, glancing past her. "The both of you."

Alia averted her eyes. Casey hung her head and followed the nurse. What choice did she have?

Perhaps in another situation, she would have tried to argue, but her mortal fear for her father had bled the last bit of fight out of her.

She trudged downstairs after the nurse. Sure enough, she led them to Ms. Pravada's office. The girls were politely encouraged to sit down, which they did.

Ms. Pravada interlaced her hands on her desk and took a

deep breath. "We have all had a trying day." That was an understatement. "But there is a little matter, unrelated to today's news, that we must clear up. First of all, you both must know that while students will gossip, I do not tolerate slanderous rumors or accusations designed to hurt others."

Casey opened her mouth to object, but a raised finger from Ms. Pravada scared her back into silence.

"You will have your chance to speak, Ms. Osprey, *after* I am finished." She paused, as if daring her to interrupt again. When no one did, Ms. Pravada continued: "I do not tolerate those kinds of stories being spread around. Now, you." Those piercing dark eyes bored right into Casey. "I thought I was clear that if you ever got yourself into another uncomfortable situation, you were to come to a teacher or myself with it immediately."

Casey reluctantly nodded her agreement.

"And you." She turned her eyes on Alia. "We have already have *several* conversations about lying, and if it turns out—"

"I wasn't ly—"

"I'm not finished." Ms. Pravada took a deep breath. "*If* it turns out that any part of what you told me was a fabrication, you already know what the consequences will be."

Lying? Casey wondered. *Consequences?* What would Alia have to lie about? She'd always been honest with Casey… hadn't she?

"Now, despite everything, I am willing to hear you both out, because these accusations are quite serious. And because what you told Mrs. Mora, and what Alia told me seem to align, at least on the main points. So, we are all here now. Let's get the story straight. Who would like to go first?"

The world seemed to tilt on its axis. Her mind churned until she realized what Ms. Pravada was implying about Alia. Her disbelief had fogged up her reason, and her brain took a minute to catch up, but she had arrived now, and the conclusion was outrageous.

"I can't believe it," Casey said. "You actually told her?"

Casey sought her friend's face. Alia just slunk low in her chair and refused to look in her direction.

"Even after we talked about it? I told you I would think of something. That I would deal with it *my* way."

"Renata can't be allowed to get away with it!" Alia burst out. "So I told Ms. Pravada for you, because it was the only way to get Stellis and Mandi to stop picking on you."

"It wasn't yours to tell! And it didn't happen to you! It happened to *me*."

"It happened to all of us, Casey. Renata's class captain for the whole school because you were too scared to—"

"Girls," Ms. Pravada said, "That's enough."

"*I* was too scared? Me? What about you? If I tattled to Ms. Pravada when Stellis and Mandi were picking on you, you would have hated me for it. You would have been too embarrassed to leave your room! And then you have the gall to go and—"

"Enough!" Ms. Pravada shouted as she shot to her feet. "That is quite enough, girls. There will be time to discuss this afterward, believe me. For now, I need to hear the full story. Facts only."

Casey realized she was standing over Alia with her fists clenched. Mrs. Mora stood in front of the door, hands clasped before her. There was no escaping this time.

Casey lowered herself back into her chair and sighed. "I can't."

"Why not?" asked Ms. Pravda.

When Casey didn't speak up, Mrs. Mora did. "Apparently, Renata stole something that belongs to Casey."

Casey turned around and glared at her. "I told you that in confidence!"

"What did she take, Casey?" Ms. Pravada asked.

"Go on," Mrs. Mora said gently.

"My Mom's holovid," she whispered. "It's the only thing I have left of hers." She wasn't about to count the ficacia tree. It was half-dead already, even if she couldn't yet bring herself to give up on it. "My Dad gave it to her as an anniversary present before I was born."

"I see," said Ms. Pravada. "And why did she take it from you?"

Not that it mattered, but what choice did she have? Casey told her the story of how she walked in on Renata, Stellis and Mandi in Mr. Hobbs classroom, manipulating numbers on his holoscreen under his account.

"How do you know they were the election numbers?"

Casey cast her mind back in memory. She had just *known.* "It wasn't like I had time to verify it. They pinned me down and threatened to kill me if I told anyone, and then took the holovid as collateral." *And now I'll probably lose it because I'm telling you all of this.*

The headmaster pursed her lips. "The thing is, Casey, we have already asked Mr. Hobbs and he tells us that his tab never left his sight that night."

"What! That's impossible. They were definitely logged in with his creds. I saw it!"

"Is it possible you were mistaken about what you saw?"

"What? No! Of course not!"

She couldn't believe it. First, Mrs. Mora didn't believe her, and now Ms. Pravada didn't either? Her mom's holovid was forever lost to her, and she didn't even get to trade it for something *good.*

"Can't you check?" Casey asked. She thought about what Alia had suggested. "Look at the history on Mr. Hobbs' tab. Surely it'll show you when he accessed the results and how he changed them. That's all the proof you need."

Frowning, Ms. Pravada picked up her HUD glasses and put them on. With a series of flicking, scrolling motions, she navigated back through the data, presumably to that very night.

"He accessed the data several times that day. We all did."

"But doesn't it show that it was *changed?*"

Ms. Pravada pulled the spectacles off and set them on the desk again. "No, it doesn't."

Casey was flabbergasted. How the hell did Renata do that? She was so sure…

Alia had remained quiet during this part of the conversation. Her face was drawn and hopeless. As angry as Casey was with her for betraying her trust and tattling to Ms. Pravada when she asked her not to, neither of them wanted Renata to get away with stealing the election.

"Even if you can't prove Renata cheated," Casey said, "surely you can't let her go unpunished for attacking me."

"It's my job to discipline my students," Ms. Pravada pointed out, "not yours."

Casey barreled onward. "Not to mention how mean Stellis and Mandi have been to me in the week since! Ask anyone, there are tons of witnesses. They've pulled pranks on me, stolen my clothes out of my locker during gym, and all sorts of other terrible shit."

"Watch your language, young lady."

"My language! How can you be so blind?"

"I am not blind, Ms. Osprey. I know very well that Stellis and Mandi are petty bullies, and that Renata Spector has become a master at manipulating people's emotions." She took a deep breath, steeling herself. It wasn't just Mr. Hobbs whose emotions were being manipulated, apparently. "Nonetheless, without evidence, I can't very well suspend her based on your accusation alone."

"I don't know how she hacked your system, but she *did*

steal my mom's holovid. For sure she did! You can't steal another student's property at Polar Prep, can you?"

"Indeed, you cannot." Ms. Pravada pinched her lips together while she thought about it. "How will I know it's yours?"

Casey told her about the osprey, and about the inscription on the underside of the disc.

"Mrs. Mora, escort these two back to their rooms and keep tabs on them while I have the security team investigate."

Casey fumed silently on the way back up to the room. By the time they got back to her dorm—Alia's was just down the hall—she couldn't hold her fury in any long. She grabbed Alia's arm and turned the shorter girl to face her. "How could you?"

Alia glanced at Mrs. Mora, who stepped discretely away but gave Casey a firm shake of her head. Casey dropped her arm.

"It seemed like a good idea at the time," Alia said. "Ms. Pravada will find something, I know she will."

"You heard her! She already said she can't prove it."

"I'm sorry, Casey." Alia's big hazel eyes brimmed with tears.

Casey felt as much pity for her as XB-9 did—which is to say, none at all. It didn't matter that Casey had told Mrs. Mora the same thing in her moment of weakness at the nurse's office. If Alia had kept her mouth shut, she could have denied it, and they wouldn't have been dragged in front of the headmaster and forced to confess.

"Sorry doesn't get my mom's holovid back." Casey swiped open the door to her dorm.

"I'm sorry, Casey," Alia said, tears running down her cheeks. "Please."

Casey slammed the door in her face.

She spent the next hour checking the feeds for any sign of

her Dad. The thought of videoing herself in this state was too horrible to bear. She couldn't bring herself to send anything more than text-based messages.

He didn't respond to any of them.

The news feeds still weren't reporting any survivors. Apparently, the Fleet had dispatched half of their warships to scour the system and do what damage they could to the Kryl. They were already talking on the newscasts like the colony was gone. Once the Kryl claimed a world and began to sink their talons into it, the planet quickly became uninhabitable to humanity. Within a couple rotations of Ariadne, it would be transformed into a Kryl hive—and lost to humanity forever.

After about an hour, another knock sounded on her dorm room door. Casey opened it to find two people from the security team, and Ms. Pravada—empty handed.

She didn't need to say anything. Casey already knew. But Ms. Pravada spoke anyway. "We searched Renata's dorm room, and her locker, and the rooms and lockers of Stellis and Mandi and several of their friends. I'm sorry to tell you this, but we didn't find your mom's holovid anywhere."

"Either she's hidden it somewhere, or she's already thrown it in the snow and it's ruined."

"I'm sorry, Casey. I do believe you're telling me the truth, you know. But without proof… It's out of my hands."

"Thanks for trying, I guess."

Ms. Pravada gave her a tight smile. "Hang in there. If we get word about your father, I'll be sure to let you know."

Of course Ms. Pravada was tracking her father's movements. Maybe that's why she was going out of her way to prove Casey right. She felt guilty that, in all likelihood, Casey had lost her father today.

Both her parents gone within months of each other.

This was the worst year of her life.

When she looked up again, Ms. Pravada, Mrs. Mora, and the security team were walking away.

Alia, who had been sitting with her knees clutched to her chest in the hallway, pushed herself to her feet. Tear-streaks stained her face. Her mouth worked a few times, like a fish out of water. "I'm so sorry, Casey. Please, forgive me. I never wanted to hurt you."

"Well, you did."

"I'm so sorry. Please. Please." Her voice cracked as she sobbed. Other students had come out of their rooms and were peering down the hallway.

"I don't ever want to see you again, Alia. You're dead to me."

Casey shut the door in her former friend's face.

SEVEN

T hey were supposed to have school the next morning, but Casey woke to a notification on her tab that classes had been cancelled. The Emperor had declared a day of mourning on Ariadne for the loss of Yuzosix.

Casey lay in bed for a long time, lost in her thoughts. The grief of losing her father weighed on her like a second gravity, pulling her down, making her limbs heavy and sitting like a bot on her chest. She alternated between crying softly, aching longingly, and being overcome with a desperate anger. Her Dad could be such a heartless jerk sometimes, but dammit, she missed him so much.

She thought of her mother and him together. How happy they'd once been—how happy they'd all been, as a family, before her mom got sick. At least with her mom, she'd been able to say goodbye. At least with her mom, there had been weeks of a slow decline for Casey to grow accustomed to the idea of losing her. It didn't make it any easier—but she had cherished that time. She had known while it was happening that she needed to treasure every moment like it was her last.

It was different with her Dad. He had been stolen from her by the Kryl. She never got to say goodbye.

She wasn't ready to now. But that's how life was. Things came at you when you least expected them. They hit you hard and left you reeling.

It was nearly the end of the lunch hour when she finally got disgusted enough with her lethargy to roll out of bed. She'd skipped dinner last night, and it felt like her stomach was beginning to devour itself. She knew she wouldn't be able to find any hot food until dinner if she missed lunch, so Casey made her way downstairs in search of something to eat.

A hundred or so students were scattered around the dining hall, about a quarter of the room's capacity, leaving plenty of tables open. She scanned the room, looking for Alia, but she didn't find her. Nor did she spot Renata, Mandi or Stellis. Satisfied that the coast was clear, she ordered two grilled cheese sandwiches and a big bowl of tomato soup—comfort food, like her mom used to make for her when she was feeling under the weather—and sat at an empty table by herself.

She tore through the sandwiches and was slurping the last of the lukewarm soup out of her bowl when Stellis and Mandi strolled lazily behind her, making little "cheep, cheep" sounds.

Her heart fluttered, but Casey refused to give them the satisfaction of reacting. She had been bullied by them enough now to know that they got off on her fear, loving nothing more than to see her squirm. Also, that the less she reacted, the less terrible the torment would ultimately be. The more stoic and brave she acted—even when she was petrified inside—the sooner they would grow bored and leave her alone.

It worked this time. When she didn't react, they walked off, laughing softly and whispering to each other.

Casey lifted the bowl to her face and drained the last of the soup. When she lowered it, Renata was sitting on the bench seat across the table from her.

Oh, Earth, she thought. But Casey refused to be intimidated, and stubbornly held her ground. Now that her mom's holovid was gone, Renata had no real power over her.

Then why are you still so terrified?

"Hey, little bird."

"What do you want, Renata?"

"I came to express my condolences." She sighed heavily and dropped her shoulders, as if the very thought had been a burden to her. "I heard your father was on a mission on Yuzosix."

How did she hear that? Alia must have been running her mouth again when she shouldn't have. Casey couldn't believe she ever trusted that girl with anything.

"Thanks, I guess," Casey said.

"And… I'm sorry. We really got off on the wrong foot, didn't we?"

Casey blinked. What was even happening? Was Renata really *apologizing* to her?

"Sorry for what, exactly?" she asked as she set the empty soup bowl down between them, in case she should need something to use as a makeshift shield.

"For letting Mandi and Stellis give you such a hard time, for starters. They can be a bit… overzealous, you know? They're loyal—to a fault—and I fear you got caught in the crossfire."

"There was no crossfire. I was the only one they were aiming at."

Renata glanced across the dining hall to where Stellis and Mandi were now tormenting another young student—a boy of about fifteen years old who was late to hit puberty. He was furiously studying his shoes. Casey could imagine the kinds of things they were saying to him. Stellis grabbed his hand and rested it on her breast. He blushed bright red and yanked his hand away, and Mandi threw her head back, cackling,

"Still, I feel bad about it," Renata said.

"Is this some kind of trick? You want to get back at me for telling Ms. Pravada about… about what you did."

"What exactly did I do, little bird?" Renata asked, fluttering her eyelashes.

Casey scowled. "You know what." She glanced pointedly down at the Polar Prep class captain's badge pinned on her uniform shirt, over her heart.

"I won that election fair and square," she said.

Casey felt her brows furrow. She twisted to look back at Stellis and Mandi, but they weren't paying attention to Renata and Casey's conversation.

"But regardless, no, this isn't to get back at you for anything. Ms. Pravada did what she had to do, just like you did what you had to do. It wasn't your fault Alia went and ran her mouth again… is it?"

"No," Casey said.

"I didn't think so. She's kind of a tattletale. You shouldn't have told her anything about what we discussed in the first place, but… you're friends, so that can be forgiven."

"We *were* friends."

Renata nodded sadly. "I figured as much. She's… a hard person to like. You'd have known that if you'd been around longer, but you're still pretty new here. You don't know how things work at Polar Prep yet."

She was starting to learn. Slowly, and each lesson cost her, but she was learning.

"So… do you accept my apology, little bird?"

"I hate that name."

"Of course you do. You're supposed to. It's a nickname."

That left a horrible taste in Casey's mouth, but she tried her best not to show it. "Why should I accept your apology?"

"Because I said I'm sorry, for starters," Renata said, looking offended.

"Not good enough," Casey said. "You and your 'friends' have been making my life miserable. And you never returned my mom's holovid. I don't know how you kept it hidden from Ms. Pravada, but I want it back."

Did she say "want"? Her desire for her mom's holovid was more in the category of *need*, but she wasn't about to give that card up to Renata so easily. She was being awful nice right now, but Casey still didn't trust her.

"You're right," Renata said, surprising Casey yet again. "If you accept my apology, I'll make sure you get the holovid back."

Her heart stopped. "Are you serious?"

"Yeah, sure. Why not?"

Casey licked her lips. "And you'll make Stellis and Mandi stop tormenting me?"

Renata shrugged. "I'll talk to them. No guarantees. They do their own thing."

Casey thought they'd do whatever Renata told them to do, but she didn't want to press her luck.

"Okay, fine. I forgive you. Now where's my mom's holovid?"

"Meet me in the girl's locker room after dinner, and we'll go get it together."

"This better not be a trick."

"No trick. I just don't have it with me. I put it somewhere for safekeeping. But I can't get it by myself, I need your help."

"Why should I do that?"

"I suppose I could just ask Stellis or Mandi to help me instead…"

"Fine," Casey said. "I'll be there."

Renata rapped her knuckles on the table. "Great! Glad we had this conversation, little bird. I want things to be right between us."

Casey didn't know about that, but she'd do just about anything to get her mom's holovid back. As Renata turned away, Casey gathered her dishes and began to walk over to return them to the kitchen.

"Oh," Renata said, circling back. "Forgot to tell you. Dress warm."

She was gone before Casey could object.

By the time Casey reached the locker room, she was already sweating through her synthweave. It had been dark for hours, and the only lights on in the locker room were for emergencies. It gave the slick tile floor, long mirrors, and rows of rockers a dim, creepy feel.

Her skin itched, and not just from being overdressed.

"Hey, little bird."

Casey jumped. Renata was sitting on the bench near the back door that led out to the sports fields, lacing up her snow boots.

"I was starting to think you decided not to come."

She almost didn't, but wasn't going to give Renata the satisfaction of knowing that. "Had to get my synthweave shirt from the laundry."

"You ready?"

Casey pulled on her parka and zipped it up, then dug her mittens and hat out of the pockets. "Where are we going?"

"You'll see."

Casey swallowed a sigh and trailed the taller girl out the back door and into the cold.

The wind burned her cheeks as they forged a path across the practice pitch and track, both buried in dry snow drifts. She began to follow a packed path on the other side of the track, the trail students ran a few times a week for their daily exercise. This morning was the only weekday morning she hadn't run the trail since she got to Polar Prep, since they'd cancelled the students' regular fitness regimen along with their classes.

"They gave us the day off so we didn't have to run this trail, you know."

"Just be glad we're walking. At least it's already packed down."

Casey grunted.

At least it was a cloudless night. With Ariadne's moon reflecting off the snow, they had plenty of light to travel by.

The fitness regimen had made her strong. The path angled up into the foothills, but it wasn't hard going. Her lungs were used to breathing in the cold air, and for once she was actually thankful for the training Polar Prep required of every student. They said that fitness was a key component of military readiness, and since this was a military prep academy, it was important that they learned the discipline now they would need later, once they were old enough to enlist, or were qualified to proceed to officer training.

Renata made small talk while they walked, asking Casey about what it was like growing up on Ariadne. Being from Oltanis, she never got to visit the capital planet's main urban centers—where the Osprey manor was located, close to Parliament and the headquarters of other government agencies. Out on the colony worlds, they hadn't had to ration food and water to support the population, and Renata was still curious about how that worked. Students of Polar Prep were insulated from it. To Casey, rationing was just the way of things, however, Renata's questions revealed how little she actually knew about the logistics, since dealing with rations was something her parents took care of for her.

"What do you want to do in the Fleet?" Renata asked, changing the topic. "When they finally let you join up."

Casey screwed up her face. "I don't know. I never wanted to be military."

"Then what are you even doing here?"

"My Dad made me come."

"Huh. I guess that explains why you hate it so much."

"I don't hate it… I just, what's the point of spending your life fighting the Kryl?" She didn't dare tell Renata the *real* reason she didn't want to join the campaign against the Kryl. She hadn't even told Alia when they were at their closest. She couldn't bear the thought of giving her life to the cause that took her mother—the reason she got cancer in the first place. "It never ends."

"You don't think fighting for peace in the galaxy is a worthy cause?"

A cause that has already taken so much from me? First Mom, and now Dad, too. "It's just…" Casey didn't trust her voice. She felt tears coming on and refused to cry in front of Renata. Thank Animus for the biting wind blowing out of the foothills that froze the tears coming to her eyes. She shook her head.

"I worked my ass off to get here, you know," Renata said. "When I was your age, I was studying late to get the best grades, applying to a dozen different scholarships each week. By the time I was fourteen I had done more extracurricular activities than most upperclassmen will do by the time they graduate. There aren't any military prep academies on Olaris, but they finally agreed to let me into Polar Prep on Ariadne. It changed my life."

What do you know about a changed life? That's what Casey

wanted to say. Instead, she asked, "You've only been here for a few years?"

"Five years. I'm a year or two older than most upper-classmen."

That explained her womanly figure, and her level of maturity. So why in all the Earth-blasted hells was she leading Casey into the mountains after dark to find her mom's holovid?

"How much farther?" Casey asked.

"Not far."

They were approaching the obstacle course where the older students pushed their physical training to new limits, imitating the bootcamp that all new SDF soldiers would have to endure. There were ladders, wooden walls, high-climbing rope swings, all arranged in a zig-zag pattern that circled back on itself so the groups could proceed through the course in laps.

Casey's grade wasn't required to do the obstacle course yet, as most of them were too small for it. She'd observed as some of the older kids did it, and itched to test herself—while also being nervous about it. It seemed really difficult, and injuries were common. What if she went up on one of those high ropes and fell off? It would be an awful long way for a person to fall, and while the dry snow provided some cushion, a thick layer of ice was hidden beneath.

A crunch sounded behind her. Casey turned, frowning, but found only snowdrifts and the packed path up which they'd come.

"All right," Renata said, "I hid the holovid up in the sniper's nest."

Casey followed her gaze up to the tippy top of a spindly tower—the highest point of the high-ropes course. The sniper's nest was nothing more than a small platform ringed by a waist-high metal rail. To get up there in the first place, the ropes course racer had to hang from a rope and pull themselves across, supported only by a harness attached to a pulley.

"What?" Casey asked. "Why?" This was her brilliant hiding spot? The idea gobsmacked her.

"Because no one would ever think to look there for it—if they could even get up there in the first place."

Even among the upperclassmen, not all of the students were strong enough or brave enough to make it. Although, unless they had a valid medical excuse, they had to do it at least once to graduate. Renata wasn't one of those. Casey had seen her reach the sniper's nest on more than one occasion.

"All right," Casey said, crossing her arms and shivering against the chill, "so I'll wait down here while you go get it."

"No can do, little bird. I'm not tall enough to get it by myself. It's way up there, taped to the back of the pole. Once we're in the nest, I'll need to boost you up to get it down."

Casey's breath formed a cloud around her head as she let out an exasperated sigh. She knew for certain that if she turned away, she'd never see that holovid again. The osprey hologam was the only thing better than a memory she had left of her mother's. She'd come this far. Couldn't turn back now and live with herself.

"Fine," she said.

Renata shot her a smile. "Good. It'll be fun."

The older girl pulled a harness out of her parka and tossed it to Casey. She shook her head. Where had she gotten this? It was a bit big for Casey, but she could tighten up the leg straps and it would do fine.

Renata stopped at the bottom of the ropes course and began to step into a harness of her own.

Before she could object, they were climbing. Casey didn't have time to be scared. She followed Renata across a rope net, and then up a straight line to a low nest—exactly like the sniper's nest, but only a few meters off the ground—before she could object.

Casey's boot slipped through a hole in the ice-slicked rope. She caught herself, hanging on.

"Come on, keep up!" Renata said.

Casey made a frustrated sound in her throat, but tried to move quicker.

When they reached the place where harnesses were required, Renata showed her how to use the locking carabiner to clip onto the safety line, which was strung overhead. They each had a pair of carabiners on the harness, extended by short daisy chains with multiple loops you could adjust based on your height and the position of the line. One carabiner kept you secure and safe, while the other was for backup. Two points of failure provided redundancy.

"You always have to have one clipped in," Renata said. "That way if you slip while you're switching lines, you won't fall to the ground."

"Makes sense," Casey said, swallowing. She wished she brought some water with her, but she hadn't thought they were going this far. She wiped her mitten along a railing and then licked the snow off it. Not exactly sanitary, but it helped a little.

"Almost there," Renata said, her cheeks red, her voice breathless.

Casey could tell how much she loved the thrill of the climb. That thrill was infectious. Casey found herself smiling and climbing hard, the cold forgotten, as they switched safety lines to the final stretch. Renata spun around and hooked her ankles around the last rope. She began to haul herself up the angled line, hand over hand, toward the sniper's nest.

Casey swallowed her fear and hooked her carabiners to the new line. But she was too short to grab the rope. She could just barely touch the line with her fingertips if she stood on her tiptoes.

"I can't reach!" Casey called.

"Yes, you can!" Renata had to shout to be heard over the wind. It was strong enough up here to sway the rope like a pendulum. "Stand on the railing to boost yourself up."

Casey felt the whole contraption tilt to the side as a strong gust blew in from her right. She grabbed for the railing, but missed, and fell beneath it as her feet slipped on the slick metal surface.

Only the carabiners attached to the safety line above arrested her fall.

"Are you serious?" Casey said as she hauled herself back up, her whole body shaking.

"You didn't fall, did you?"

"Almost!"

"See? The carabiners and the harness caught you." Renata said as she finally reached the sniper's nest and righted herself, sliding into the safety of the small platform and its pathetic railing. "So now you know you're perfectly secure."

Casey steeled herself, putting one foot up, but as she tried to shift her weight, feeling her foot slip, she panicked and sank back to the platform.

"I can't do it!"

"Come on, little bird. This is the only way to get that holovid back!"

Casey took a deep, shuddering breath. For her Mom. She could do it for her Mom.

Don't think about it. Just go!

She put her foot up on the railing again, levering herself up—and got the line in her mittens. She swapped the carabiners over, one at a time. Then she turned herself backwards, like she'd seen Renata do, and hooked her ankles over the line. Slowly, ever so slowly, she began to pull herself across the gap, nothing but empty air below and only two measly metal clips to keep her from falling.

Her arms were so tired. As she hauled herself across, her muscles began to burn. The damned line was angled at a slight incline so that she was actually pulling her whole body weight uphill against gravity. Her numb fingers began to lose their power to grip anything.

"Nearly there!" Renata said. "Two more pulls!"

Casey took a deep breath, reached out, and heaved.

"Last one!" Renata was practically screaming into her ear. She was close, then!

Casey slid her mittened hands up the line for one last pull —and her feet slipped off. The weight of her body ripped her off the rope and she dropped, screaming.

The harness snapped tight around her thighs, cinching up —and something caught her daisy chains. Renata pulled her the rest of the way to the sniper's nest.

"Good job, little bird!" She hauled Casey into the sniper's nest and hooked first one, then the other, carabiner to the central pole, securing her in place. "I'm actually pretty impressed. I think it took me two or three tries to make that. You nearly did it on the first run."

Casey breathed deeply of the frigid air. Her whole body shook with adrenaline. "I thought I was a goner there for a second."

"You would have been fine. That's what the harness is for."

"Still. Frightening." She gave a little chuckle.

"You're not wrong. Okay, the last part is the easy bit," Renata said. She cupped her hands below her waist. "Come around this side and step into my hands."

Casey did. Her daisy chains stretched just far enough to stand up in Renata's hand. Renata lifted her up to reach a small handhold about three feet above the older girl's head.

"Hang onto that for a second, would you? I need to adjust my grip."

Casey did as she was told. "I don't see it!"

There was a clicking sound as Renata adjusted her own carabiners.

"Where's the holovid? I thought you said it was taped up here."

"I lied."

"What?!" Casey said. She let go of the handle to drop back to the surface of the platform—and found herself stuck, suspended with her feet dangling above the height of the railing.

Renata hadn't moved *her own* carabiners. She'd moved Casey's to an O-ring up above the level of the safety line—so Casey was stuck, a meter and a half above the platform, with her weight in her harness.

"What do you think you're doing?" Casey demanded.

Renata pulled the disc of the holovid out of an inside pocket in her parka. "You wanted this, right? Of course you do, I can see it in your eyes."

"You had it in your pocket the whole time?" Casey shouted. "Why the hell did you make me climb all the way up here?!"

Renata pitched the disc over the side of the platform, where it disappeared into a snow drift ten meters—or more —below. It left a small dent in the smooth white mound.

Renata began to clip herself to the safety rope to return the way they'd come.

"Don't leave me here!"

She ignored Casey's plea.

"Why are you doing this, Renata?"

"So you can hang out up here like the stupid little bird you are and think about what you did. Sicking Ms. Pravada on me was a bad idea. She didn't catch me, but Earth… it was too close, Osprey. I told you, I'd make your life miserable if you told anyone what you saw. Next time, you'll think twice before you try to fuck with me. I don't let anyone get in my way—especially not spoiled little brats like you."

"You're going to pay for this, Renata!"

"I doubt," Renata said. "But if I do, it'll be worth it."

Casey glanced down. Mandi and Stellis were standing on the trail, pointing up at her and laughing to each other. They'd followed them up here.

"Renata! Don't leave me here! *RENATA!*"

The older girl ignored her as she slid down the safety line and quickly made her way to the ground. She bumped fists with Mandi and Stellis, and the three of them made their way back to the school, leaving Casey hanging there in the frozen night.

EIGHT

Casey hung there, berating herself for being such a trusting fool, for longer than she wanted to admit.

Then she decided it was time to take matters into her own hands.

Renata had secured her well. The only real danger up here was the cold. But she was dressed for it. However, unless she freed herself, they'd find her here, shivering, in eight hours when the upperclassmen went on their morning training run.

She didn't intend to let that happen. It was embarrassing enough to be stuck up here in the first place. She didn't want anyone to find her.

That left her only one option. She would climb down, recover her mom's holovid from that snowdrift, then hurry back to the school where she could plot her revenge.

Earth damn Renata! That petty bitch. She would pay for this.

Casey's anger was so distracting. What would her mom have done in this situation? Or her father?

Focus on the problem, she told herself. *One step at a time. That's what they would have done.*

The first step, of course, was to reposition the safety clips. Renata had latched her carabiners to an O-ring or something on the opposite side of the pole, out of her reach. Casey leaned around to one side, and then the other. The pole wasn't too thick. Her mittens could just barely brush the curved sides of the metal carabiners. However, she couldn't get a good grip on them with the thick padding of her mittens in the way.

Maybe she could get her fingers around them and release one if she took a mitten off. She grabbed the synth-weave in her teeth and slid one off. Blast, but it was cold! She hadn't realized how much protection the mitten provided. Good thing she didn't have to keep it off for long.

She had to lean way out to reach the carabiner, but she *was* able to get her fingers around it. The clip was tight, though, the oblong shape pulled hard against the central pole of the sniper's nest due to her weight sitting in her harness. Renata had cinched up the daisy chains as tight as they would go. In order to unclip the carabiner, she'd have to reduce the load on her harness.

Casey kicked back with her feet until her toes found the icy railing ringing the sniper's nest. She could just barely reach it. She stretched her toes, releasing some of her weight from the carabiners, which allowed her to squeeze the release lever. It worked! She managed to slide the first cara-biner off the O-ring.

That left her in the precarious position of having only one carabiner supporting her weight, keeping her from falling.

She looked for something to hook the loose carabiner onto, to provide the safety of redundancy, but stuck in this position, well above the railing and still dangling on the opposite side of the safety line she used to reach the nest, there was nothing useful that the daisy chain could actually be attached to.

Taking a deep breath, Casey decided to risk it. It would only be for a moment. She shuffled around until she was well within reach of the second carabiner, using the railing below as a thin edge to walk on. She unhooked the second carabiner and, as her full weight came down, felt her boots slip.

The railing came up to meet her face with alarming speed. Her jaw slammed into the ice-covered metal bar, splashing black and red splotches across her vision. There was a clang of metal as the carabiners rebounded off the pole, or maybe the railing, or maybe the platform below. Casey was too disoriented to know which. She reached out, grabbing for anything she could hang onto, but it was too slippery to hang on.

Her body bounced off the sniper's nest and spun into the open air. She plummeted to the ground. As the cold wind whipped over her face, Casey forced her eyes open. The black and red spots cleared as a snowbank rushed up to meet her. Somehow she managed to get her boots pointed down toward the snowdrift. They came in at an angle, disappearing into the snowdrift. She reached back with her arms to break her fall.

Her left wrist hit something solid and immovable hidden in the snow beneath her.

SNAP.

The sound reverberated through her whole body, followed by a juddering, trembling sensation. Casey screamed. She couldn't feel her left arm except as a blur of pain. She rolled to her back in the snowdrift, groaning and crying, and writhed like that for a moment—for several moments—she didn't know how long exactly.

When she finally caught her breath, and came to her senses enough to raise her wrist and appraise it herself, she found her forearm bent at an unnatural angle. Casey painstakingly drew the sleeve of her parka up and found that both of the bones in her forearm had broken. Her wrist was angled unnaturally close to her elbow. There was a bulge on the opposite side of her forearm where the bones pressed against her skin. One had broken through, and there was blood—so much blood.

She pulled the sleeve back down with a hiss of pain. The mitten she'd taken off lay a few feet away. Casey crawled over on her knees and grabbed it, then slid it painfully back onto her left hand to protect her fingers from frostbite.

The holovid. With her good arm, Casey searched the snowbank. It felt like she was there for hours, grasping in the ice with numb fingers, but eventually she found it. Thank Animus the snow was dry and it was too cold to turn to water. The disc didn't seem damaged. It wouldn't turn on— probably the battery was dead—but it was in one piece, and the engraving was there on the bottom, proving that it was, indeed, her mom's.

Panting from the effort and the pain, her mouth parched from thirst and terror, Casey lumbered to her feet and began to trudge back toward the school.

It was the longest walk of her life, and the loneliest she'd ever felt. Casey had thought, on the way up with Renata, that recovering her mom's holovid would make her feel better. But it didn't. Not really.

Thoughts of vengeance lent a little warmth. No more than a spark. She was glad she recovered the holovid, sure, but it was a superficial happiness. It wouldn't bring her mother or father back.

Would she even survive without them? Or would she wither and die, like that leafless ficacia up in her room? She hadn't given a thought to her father's estate, but for some reason now the idea that she'd inherit everything he owned redoubled her grief.

Casey managed to slip back into school unseen through the locker room, the same way they'd left. Thankfully, Renata and the other girls weren't there waiting for her. It was long after curfew, and she had to tread carefully to avoid the teachers who took turns patrolling the halls at night. Casey used the back ways to avoid notice. She didn't want anyone to find and confiscate the holovid—knowing Ms. Pravada, she'd demand Casey lay out every detail of this whole awful night. Sharing this with Ms. Pravada wouldn't solve anything. It would only make the problem worse, yet again. No, Casey would get her revenge on Renata. But she'd get it *her* way.

Still, her broken arm needed to be treated, and she would have to go to the nurse's office for that, but first she had to get rid of the evidence of her nighttime outing, and fabricate a story about how she broke it.

Casey made it to her dorm room, where she dropped off the holovid and her synthweave layers without incident, using her good hand to change into sweatpants and a t-shirt. From there, she headed back down to the nurse's office.

To her surprise, instead of a night-shift nurse, she found Mrs. Mora still working alongside Ms. Pravada.

"Casey?" Mrs. Mora said, her hand going to her chest. "Did someone tell you?"

Ms. Pravada stood. "What happened to your face? Oh Animus, your arm!"

She hid it behind her back. "Tell me what?"

Mrs. Mora looked at the headmaster.

"Sit down, child," Ms. Pravada said, guiding her to a seat.

The panic she'd barely kept at bay since the attack on Yuzosix clawed out of her throat. "Just tell me!" she shouted.

"Sit down and I will."

Casey obeyed. "What happened? Is it my Dad?"

She feared the worst. Despite everything, she still held out hope that he'd somehow survived the invasion. The Kryl had killed her mother, and the thought of them taking both parents was too much to bear.

"No, dear," Ms. Pravada said. "Still no news on that front. This is about Alia. We found her in her room. She tried to commit suicide earlier tonight. Now, let me see your arm."

NINE

All petty thoughts of vengeance evaporated from her head the moment she knew her friend's life was in danger.

Yes—her friend. She'd been furious with Alia. She'd said unforgivable things. But that didn't matter now.

The headmaster insisted on setting the break and casting it immediately. Mrs. Mora administered the stitches herself, which was more painful than the initial break had been.

Casey refused to say more than "I fell" when they questioned her about what happened. Ms. Pravada gave her many suspicious looks, but Casey kept her lips pinched in a firm line and, thankfully, the headmaster let her hang onto her secrets.

The cast had hardened when they finally let Casey see Alia. The girl was sound asleep, and Casey was given firm instructions *not* to wake her. To let her rest. Alia had been given drugs to help her sleep anyway, so nothing Casey did or said would bring her back to consciousness.

When they tried to escort Casey back to her room, she

flat out refused to budge. She sank onto the floor like a stubborn toddler.

"I'm staying here. I don't care what you say."

"Dear," Mrs. Mora said, "she needs to rest. And so do you. You can see her tomorrow morning."

"I'm not leaving her. You said yourself, she's so doped up she can't hear us anyway." It was true. They spoke in quiet voices in her room, and Alia didn't so much as stir. "I'll let her rest, I promise."

Surprising Casey, Ms. Pravada left the room and returned with a comfortable padded chair. Casey sank into it.

She had every intention of staying awake. However, the night had been traumatic for her as well, and though she fought to stay conscious, eventually sleep came.

She woke with a start as the sun rose to illuminate the snow-covered mountain, which was visible through the window. She couldn't escape the sight of those foothills and the majestic peak rising like a doomed starship behind them. She was grateful, at least, for the clear sunny sky that, for once, burned away the gloom of this place.

Alia shifted in her bed and groggily rubbed at her eyes. When she saw Casey, she shoved her bandaged wrists under the sheet to hide them and the lacerations they undoubtedly covered. Her face was worn and hollow, pale, and filled with shame.

"Casey," Alia said, her voice hoarse and groggy. "What are you doing here?"

"Making sure you're okay. It's good to see you awake."

"I thought you said you didn't ever want to see me again."

"I was wrong. I spoke those words in anger. I didn't mean it." She swallowed—the saliva slithered down her throat with her stupid pride. "I'm really sorry, Alia. This is my fault."

"You didn't hold the razor, did you?"

"Might as well have." Those scars on the tops of Alia's

thighs, high enough to be hidden by her skirt, were sure signs of former self-harm. Casey should have known better. She should have *been* better. "I'm so sorry. I hope we can still be friends."

Alia frowned as her eyes traveled down to Casey's cast. "You mean that?"

"Of course I do."

Alia's frown flattened out, then blossomed into a smile to rival the sunshine. "What happened to your arm?"

"Couldn't let you show me up now, could I?"

Alia barked a laugh even as she blushed. "No, really."

She told Alia the story she'd kept from the headmaster. How Renata had baited her with promises of her mom's holovid, then betrayed her and left her hanging in the sniper's nest in the freezing cold. How she'd gotten free, then slipped and broken both her ulna *and* her radius before recovering the holovid.

She also told her how all vengeful plots to expose and crucify Renata for what she'd done had vanished the moment Casey heard Alia was in danger.

"You don't mean that."

"I do. I don't care about Renata or Mandi or Stellis anymore. Bullies like them get off on the power they hold over you. But they only have power if you *give* it to them. I know the things they've done are wrong, but I'm not giving them that power over me anymore. They can beat me up and pull stupid pranks on me if they want to, but when I don't react they'll get bored and eventually they'll give up. From now on, I'm not even going to speak their names out loud."

"When did you get so wise?"

"When I realized friends mattered a whole lot more than enemies. Only one of them adds value to a person's life."

Not to mention that Ms. Pravada had been right, after all. That was the power of her suggestion to fetch an adult rather than engage with those bullies. The moment Casey picked a fight with Mandi and Stellis, she revealed that they'd captured her attention. It was over before it had started. She wouldn't make that mistake again.

The days passed slowly as Alia recovered and started seeing a therapist. School ended up being cancelled for that whole week as the teachers and administrators of Polar Prep dealt with the fallout of the invasion of Yuzosix. Although it happened in another solar system, the ripples had catastrophic effects here at home.

Alia didn't have family on Yuzosix, and Casey needed the distraction, so they spent their time playing games and talking about inconsequential things.

Casey was dealing another hand when a thought occurred to her. "Alia, do you know what you want to be when you finally get to join the Fleet?"

Alia pursed her lips and gazed out the window. The color had returned to her face and she was feeling much better now that she'd had a few days to recover. The therapy really seemed to be working. "I think… an engineer or mechanic of some kind. I want to fix things, like bots or starfighters, you know? The bigger the better. That way people can't just tear it down. What about you?"

Casey had never really given it much thought until Renata posed the question to her. She still wasn't sure. "My mom was a xenobiologist, you know. She studied the Kryl." She'd never told anyone else at school about this. "That was how she got cancer. Whatever the Kryl do to grow and reproduce gives off a kind of radiation we still have trouble detecting and protecting our scientists from."

"Oh, Casey, I'm so sorry. That's terrible."

Casey forced a smile. "At least she died doing what she loved. It wasn't just the Kryl she studied but all manner of creatures and plants wherever they grew. It had been years since she studied the Kryl… she retired from the SDF after I was born. But she got sick from her exposure anyway."

"That's why you brought that ficacia to school with you, isn't it?" Alia asked, nodding at the plant. Casey had brought it down into the hospital room and set it by the window. It still didn't have any leaves, but it was the only plant in the room and it went a long way to giving the place some life.

"Yeah," Casey said. "It reminds me of her. She loved plants so much."

"So you want to be a xenobiologist, like her?"

"I… I don't think so," Casey said. "As you can see from the state of that plant, I don't really have the talent for it."

They both laughed.

"So, what then?" asked Alia.

Casey thought about her father. He was a soldier. He was tough, he could fight, and during his time in the service he'd made a positive impact on so many people's lives.

She didn't ever want to be an Inquisitor—the idea of holding other people's lives in her hands frightened her. She didn't want that kind of responsibility. But Casey was good with people, and she had good eyes and fast reaction times.

"I want to be a starfighter pilot."

Saying it out loud felt *good*. Better than she expected. She hadn't known it until she said it, but it was true. She did want that.

Her path at Polar Prep transformed before her. There were classes she'd need to take—training she'd need to do. She set her excitement aside. There would be plenty of time for that later. For now, she focused on Alia. On making sure she got healthy again.

"You'll be good at that," Alia said. "Especially as a squad leader. You really know how to build people up."

Casey grinned. "You think so?"

"Yeah. I really do."

Casey finished dealing the cards. "You go first this time."

There was one more thing Casey had to do. While Alia was napping—she still got tired easily, and needed lots of rest—Casey retrieved her tab from her dorm room and sat in the corner, next to the ficacia tree, while she drew from memory.

She had a passable sketch of an osprey within a few minutes, and spent the next hour sharpening the lines and getting the beak and wings just right. Alia got up at some point and went to the bathroom.

She ran back into the room a few minutes later, breathless, her face shining with barely contained eagerness.

"Casey!" she shouted. "Did you see? Did you see?!"

"See what?" Casey said.

"They found survivors! Dozens of Mammoth longhaulers and a few Fleet destroyers carrying refugees. They were just hiding with their power off to avoid detection by the Kryl until they got out of range! Ariadne is sending a rescue mission as we speak."

Casey had muted her notifications while she was drawing so she wasn't interrupted by depressing newsfeed articles about the invasion. Now, she switched them back on and was flooded with a dozen different pings.

She scrolled through them, her heart pounding. She stopped. With a shaking hand, she brought up the video she'd received via ansible less than twenty minutes ago.

"Casey," said a disheveled hologram of her father, projected into the air before her. "I'm sorry I didn't return your messages until now. The destroyer where I was deployed was orbiting Yuzosix when the Kryl executed a surprise attack. We scrambled to speed up the evacuation, and then went dark to avoid destruction when the destroyer was full. I just want you to know that I'm safe and I'll be home soon. We're out of range of a retaliatory attack now, and the rescue mission is already on its way. We have to shut the power off again momentarily. I've got to go. I'll let you know the moment we touch down on Ariadne. I just wanted to say I love you. I'm so proud of you, even if you're still mad at me for sending you to Polar Prep— well, now you see why. May Animus keep you safe."

Casey clutched the tab to her chest as Alia put an arm around her and hugged her tight. She was determined not to cry—but the sight of a new, green bud on the ficacia tree cut to her heart.

Which was still beating. As was her father's. It was all she ever wanted, and for the first time at Polar Prep, she felt true happiness.

———

Her father landed on Ariadne a week after her birthday and a day before winter break began at Polar Prep. He flew the ornithopter up the same day, and offered to unenroll her from Polar Prep and take her home if that's what she still wanted.

She didn't. Having chosen her path, and also knowing that quitting Polar Prep meant he would have to retire from a job he loved—a job where he got to help save thousands upon thousands of Solaran lives and make a *real* difference— she politely declined.

She finally understood what he meant by duty, honor and planet.

When she told him she'd decided to be a starfighter pilot, a grin split his beard, which had grown even more gray in her absence.

"That's wonderful," he said. "It'll be hard work though. You know that, don't you?"

"I'm not afraid of hard work."

He laughed. "Why am I not surprised? Hey, what happened to your arm?"

Her left arm was thinner than the right and she kept flexing her fist, trying to rebuild the muscle. The cast had come off on her birthday, her bones having healed quickly thanks to the help of some incredible pills Mrs. Mora prescribed her.

"I broke it," she said.

"Are you okay?"

"I am now. Dad, I want to get something… in memory of Mom."

"Okay," he said warily. "And what's that?"

"Tattoos."

"Absolutely not."

"If you don't let me get them now, I'll just get them on my sixteenth birthday."

"You only just turned thirteen!"

"Exactly. I'm practically fourteen already."

He chuckled, and then fell silent for a long moment as he studied her face. "Obstinate," he said. "Just like your father."

Now it was her turn to laugh. It was true.

"Tell me, tattoos of what?"

"Ospreys. One on each forearm, so I'm always reminded of her." Renata might be able to steal a holovid, but no one could take tattoos away from her.

He nodded solemnly, and wrapped an arm around her shoulder. "Fitting. She would have loved that."

"I thought so."

"Okay, I'll let you do it. But you have to wait until you're sixteen. Your mother would have had my head if I let you get tattoos now. But if you wait until you're sixteen, I'll pay for them."

She didn't want to wait. She wanted them *now*. Just like she wanted to be out there fighting the Kryl now. Just like she wanted to be done with Polar Prep now. Once she decided what she wanted, Casey didn't have the patience for any delay.

But that wasn't how life worked. Sometimes, especially when it came to the good things in life, you had to endure the hard things—and sometimes you had to wait.

"Okay, deal. Shake on it?"

He laughed, but solemnly shook her hand.

"I love you, kiddo."

"I love you, too, Dad."

OPERATION HEARTSTRIKE

BOOK 3

ONE

"M*ajor* Kira Miyaru."

Omar's whispered words, spiced with the minty scent of his favorite tabac, sent tingles up her spine. Beds on starships were neither plentiful nor large, but at least they were private.

"Major *Kira* Miyaru," he breathed.

She covered his mouth with hers, drinking in his taste and biting his lower lip.

Omar's hands trailed down her breasts and along her belly before settling on her hips. He gripped her firmly. "Major Kira *Miyaru*."

"You better watch it," she said. "I'm your commanding officer now."

"Is that right?" Omar pushed her back so that she lay beneath him.

Kira ripped off his shirt and threw it across the room. The seductive grin he gave her in response made her heart sing with joy—a feeling so rare and so fleeting in this time of interstellar conflict and xeno war that she grabbed onto it with all her might, clinging desperately.

Twisting her powerful legs, Kira rolled them both over. Now, she was on top. "I told you, I'm in charge."

She grabbed Omar's wrists and pinned them to the sheets.

"I like it when you play rough, but I think all this power is going to your head, Boss."

She laughed, then kissed him again. There wasn't much talking after that. Just a murmured word here, a moan of pleasure there.

Kira knew she had to bask in joy while it lasted. War was hell. And she'd never loved anyone like she loved Omar.

TWO

The world of Yuzosix had been their breadbasket—the Solaran Empire's largest grower of staple crops like rice, wheat and corn. It once boasted tens of thousands of greenhouses, full to bursting with exotic fruits and Earth-descended vegetables.

It was this knowledge that made Major Kira Miyaru sick to her stomach as she flew over acre after acre of the slimy, purplish-black Kryl fungus that smothered the world.

For all its arable farmland, Yuzosix itself was 90 percent water. Its aquamarine ocean still glittered in the light of the local star. From where Kira sat in the cockpit of her Scimitar, it looked as if the landmass had been scattered across a canvas of ocean by flicking paint from a brush sized for the cosmos.

Where the specks of paint landed, clusters of islands had formed, gathering here and there across both hemispheres.

Only one cluster was remotely large enough to deserve the designation of continent: a checkmark-shaped archipelago located 15 degrees south of the equator.

And even that was a stretch.

She adjusted her heading and marked the destination on her nav. With a few motions in her heads-up display, or HUD, she transmitted coordinates over broadbeam to her squad and the other groups in the strike force she was leading.

"Mark location, Banshees," she told them, "and form up on me."

She maneuvered to the head of the strike escort, positioned on either side of the bomber group, and engaged autopilot so she could take a closer look at their target.

Kira's mission briefing included a profile of Yuzosix, so she knew a massive volcano hid underwater just off the coast of the largest island. Centuries of continuous eruptions had churned the crust into a fertile bed of dark soil. That soil was the reason the archipelago had become immeasurably valuable to Ariadne and the Empire's tenuous string of colonies.

Yuzosix, alone, produced 40 percent of all grain crops distributed across Solaran space.

At least, it had. Now, it produced nothing.

Terraced cliffsides—so painstakingly sculpted by human hands to maximize the amount of productive farmland available—were no longer adorned by rice paddies and rows of green or golden crops.

Instead, a midnight-colored cancer spread across the fields. The Kryl fungus absorbed the light, seeming to swallow it with an insatiable appetite.

It was the very definition of invasive species.

This was the third world the xenos had invaded since the war began. Like the others, they claimed Yuzosix with a swiftness and ruthless brutality that boggled the mind. Those who survived the initial attacks had fled, evacuated one island at a time by the Solaran Fleet... but not before half the population had been brutally murdered. Kira had flown security or strike escort on many of those missions.

Now, she and the 2nd Fighter Squadron—nickname, Banshees—along with a massive contingent of bombers, were back to mete out the Empire's justice.

"Strike Force Delta to Command, come in Command," Kira said over tightbeam to the *Knight of Eternity*, their group's flagship destroyer.

Colonel Bo Ballerdice, Wing Commander of the 5th Fighter Wing, picked up the line. He was in charge of this operation. "This is Command, go ahead, over."

"I have visual confirmation of the archipelago. Are we clear to proceed?"

A tense silence followed her question. Kira swallowed and worked her tongue around a dry mouth. She adjusted her helmet against her spinal applicator and eyed her stim levels, the chemical scent of which she'd long ago learned to associate with focus, danger, and the frantic rush of battle.

"You're a go, Reaper. Proceed with Phase One."

Kira acknowledged the order, then signaled chaff bombers to move ahead while reducing her approach speed with the rest of the group.

She watched her lidar and radar readings as they strafed the target, dropping metal shavings designed to imitate Scimitars into the troposphere.

"Deploy Aluminite Fist," Colonel Ballerdice said.

A dozen pairs of light, supersonic starcraft dipped into the atmosphere. They moved at incredible speeds over the islands, launching precision missiles to root out the most aggressive surface-to-air defenses while the Kryl were confused by the chaff.

She flinched when a pair of starcraft blinked out on her lidar. No matter how many pilots she lost, their deaths always jolted her heart like an electric shock.

It was different now that she was commander. It hurt

more, somehow. She felt personally responsible for each life lost.

"Major Miyaru, what's happening to the chaff? Report!" Colonel Ballerdice said.

Kira checked and found a group of Kryl drones using some kind of magnetic nets to sweep it out to sea. "They've clued in to our tactics, sir. Should we return and regroup?"

Ballerdice cursed colorfully. He'd personally developed these tactics on Teviq and Joplin, the two other colonies which had been invaded as the Kryl gained ground in the war. Those worlds had been nascent colonies, younger than Yuzosix and not nearly as essential to the Solaran Empire's economy or food supply. Still, their human toll had been significant.

"Negative," said her commanding officer. "Losses are well within mission parameters. Proceed with Phase Two."

One of the reasons Kira had been awarded her new position was because the Fleet had suffered *substantial* losses over the past two years. She may have been a veteran of this war, but she was still young for a squadron commander.

The other reason was that she knew when to shut up and take orders.

Her tightbeam blinked on a private channel. She opened it and heard Omar's familiar, confident voice. "We got this, Reaper, chaff or no chaff. Put me in. I'll show you."

Ballerdice's words didn't comfort her, but Omar's did. Her resolve hardened. Out her portside window, he tilted his wings. She felt a wicked grin grow across her face.

He was the light in her darkness. Even in the face of death, Omar's presence and game attitude lifted her spirits.

If it was a fight the Kryl wanted, it was a fight they were going to get. "Frag them into oblivion, Spidermonkey," she said, using his callsign.

She switched back to Command and confirmed again—in

a more professional tone—their decision. "Proceeding with Phase Two." Then she added in a whisper, "For the people of Yuzosix."

She lowered her Scimitar's nose until it pointed at the tip of the island, then plunged into the stratosphere.

Her starfighters flew like avenging archangels. Omar blasted through Kryl drones like the destructive Spirit of Old Earth itself. They took several casualties on their way to the island chain, but not as many as they could have.

The firebombing began at the narrowest tip of the check-mark-shaped archipelago and continued across the land mass. Up close, Kira could see the fungus wasn't a continuous sheet of black-purple mold coating the ground, but broken by cracks, wrapped around steaming pools of orange-yellow sulfur, and prying open cave mouths of incipient mining sites or lairs.

None of it would survive the precision depth rounds the bomber group dropped into them. The bombs were designed to burrow into the earth, and they were aimed at every visible Kryl encroachment.

On Teviq and Joplin, their missiles hadn't gone deep enough. The Kryl protected their burrows by digging them deep—an evolutionary instinct—and the operations had to be repeated several times.

The Fleet wasn't taking any chances with this one. As they completed their first pass, two more groups were coming in behind them to repeat the process.

It made Kira sick to her stomach. There would be no Kryl left when they were done.

There would be no Yuzosix, either.

No bread basket.

Only fire and grease, smoke and destruction. No human would return to this land for decades, maybe centuries. The

Solaran Empire would have to find somewhere else to grow their crops.

Hours later, as she put the smoking wreckage in her rearview and returned to the *Knight of Eternity*, Kira held her churning gut still as she breathed through her nose and clung to the memory of joy with Omar.

It didn't solve anything—not the sickening loss of Yuzosix, not the never ending exchange of death between human and xeno—but somehow his presence made it easier to bear.

THREE

Unlike Kira, Colonel Bo Ballerdice did *not* seem to have found a way to make his suffering easier to bear.

He bared his anguish out in the open for everyone to experience.

How generous of him.

"Minister, I—" Ballerdice said before biting off his words.

Kira exchanged an uneasy glance with his adjutant. The last person to shuffle sheepishly out of the wing commander's office had left the door open a crack. As a result, they could hear this very private conversation very clearly.

"But—You see—Yes, sir, I understand the concept of collateral damage," Colonel Ballerdice could be heard saying, his tone now laced with ire.

Like everything about the man, Ballerdice's voice was loud, brash and tasteless. Even when he was defending their mission against a clueless politician who had managed to get ahold of his desk number.

"The tactics we employed on Yuzosix were cleared by the Executive Council. You do realize—"

Silence as he was interrupted again. The wing commander's adjutant, a gaunt young blond man wearing a crisply creased uniform and a standard Fleet-issued high-and-tight buzz cut, nervously straightened objects on his desk.

"I understand that, sir, but we're at war," Ballerdice said. "As I've said, the tactics we employed—No, I—sir! Sir, did you even *see* the reconnaissance photos we sent to the Defense Committee?" A pause. "Yes, I *know* that, and if we had been able to save more farmland we would have, but—Earth DAMMIT!"

Something crashed, causing the adjutant to flinch and stiffen in his seat. The poor lieutenant stared at his neatly arranged desktop with unblinking eyes under which bags, like three-day-old bruises, had formed.

"Lieutenant Peabody, my call ended early!" Ballerdice shouted from the other room, as if that were news to anybody. "What's next on my schedule?"

"Major Miyaru is here, sir."

"Well, what are you waiting for? Send her in."

Kira stepped warily into the office of Colonel Bo Ballerdice. The room was hung with holos of Ballerdice shaking hands with famous admirals, a shadow box full of medals, and an Imperial flag bearing the Tri-Star logo. Models of starfighters and other Fleet craft had been carefully positioned on shelves and at the corner of his desk.

Although he was married with kids, Kira found no holos or pictures of them in the room. She had no idea what his wife looked like, and the wing commander never spoke of his family. The decor gave the whole place a rather impersonal, bureaucratic and imposing vibe.

Seeing her gaze around caused Colonel Bo Ballerdice's chest to puff up with pride. Had he really only moved in here after they returned to Ariadne following the Yuzosix mission?

Didn't he have better things to do than decorate?

"Hello, sir," Kira said. "You asked to see me?"

"Yes, I did. I have a special assignment for you."

This whole situation was odd. It put Kira on her guard. Usually, her missions were handed down in a briefing room, alongside the other squadron commanders involved. Usually, she received a written summary ahead of time, sent directly to her tab. Neither of those things had happened today.

I should have brought a witness, Kira thought.

But she'd been told to come alone.

"Sir?" she asked.

Ballerdice's eyes glittered with secrets. "Close the door."

She did so, and then stood at attention. The wing commander sat and tapped the transparent surface of his own tab. Her ears popped and a faint whine sounded as a hidden noise suppression device activated.

"This is a top secret mission. You earned it, after the way you and your squad flew on Yuzosix."

She couldn't help but feel a swell of pride. "Thank you, sir. It's a shame what we had to do, but I'm glad we accomplished our objective."

"Yes. Animus knows we're getting flack about it." If he sounded regretful, it was only that he didn't enjoy fielding calls from angry politicians. Feeding and housing millions of displaced people was undoubtedly going to be problematic for the Empire. She knew Colonel Ballerdice had zero sympathy for refugees, or even the Empire's food production dilemma. All he seemed to care about was how much shit he had to eat because of it.

As if in answer to her silent thoughts, Ballerdice glared at his tab for a second, no doubt reminiscing over his previous conversation.

"Which is why this next mission is critical," the colonel said. "We don't want to have to burn the Kryl out of another colony, and there's only one way to make that happen."

"I'm listening, sir." The way her body was reacting to this conversation, you'd think she expected a Kryl groundling to dart out from under his mahogany desk and go for her femoral artery.

"The details have to stay between us for now."

She nodded warily.

"I need to hear you say it. This can't leak. You're to repeat what I tell you to *no one*. Not the other squadron commanders, not your flight leads, not even your lovers."

Her heart skipped a beat as chills swept across her back. Did he know about Omar? The plural made her uncertain. Did he assume she was polyamorous so as not to offend her? That would have been polite but... unlike him.

Relationships between Fleet personnel were technically allowed—how else were young, horny pilots stuck together on a starship lightyears from home for months or years at a time to vent their stress? It was easier to have a soft policy than to make busy officers spend their time trying to police natural human urges. She and Omar had started seeing each other when they were captains of different flight teams. She was abundantly aware how the situation had changed with her recent promotion, and it *was* frowned upon for commanding officers to be intimate with those they commanded. Such a thing was widely accepted to be bad for morale, as attachment always posed additional risk and complicated command decision-making. However, they didn't strictly forbid it, but dealt with those situations on a case-by-base basis.

But how had *Ballerdice* known?

She and Omar had been so careful. So private. They never, *ever* displayed any signs of affection in public. Her mind raced.

And that's when she realized that her hesitation, her very

lack of immediate response, had confirmed for Ballerdice what he'd only suspected up to now.

"You can trust me, sir," Kira rushed to say. "Whatever you tell me will stay between us."

His eyes glistened again. He knew he'd gotten the better of her.

Earth, how I despise this man, she thought.

Surprising her, Colonel Ballerdice failed to linger on his victory. "We're organizing a stealth assault on Planet K," he said. "The gearheads over at the new Ministry of Xeno Affairs have devised a weapon system they believe will be powerful enough to slay the Queen Mother."

"I thought the Kryl Overmind was buried deep undergound."

"Let's just say that those burrowing bombs they've been working on have gotten better. A *lot* better."

Her brows drew down. "But how are we even going to get close enough to Planet K to drop them?"

"You'll learn more at the briefing. Suffice to say we're devising a plan. It'll be hard, but it's viable."

She exhaled heavily. It was a frightening prospect—a mission that took her to the very heart of Kryl space would be incredibly risky.

But the reward? If they were successful, the reward would be enormous.

No more Kryl invasions.

No more refugee evacuations.

No more *war*.

She and Omar could go on vacation. On a beach. Somewhere peaceful and remote. Maybe they could even… no. She pushed the dream from her mind. It was too remote a possibility. Even *thinking* it frightened her. She tucked that idea into a dark pit in the back of her heart where it would be safe.

Where the likes of Colonel Ballerdice wouldn't be able to ruin it.

"It's risky, sir," she said.

"It is."

"We might not succeed."

"We *will*."

The flames of her hunger licked up out of the pit and warmed her. She didn't need to like this man to fight beside him. They were on the same side, after all. Kira met his eyes. "All right. What are your orders?"

He slapped his wooden desk with a powerful hand, his wedding ring making a sharp crack on impact. "That's the spirit, Miyaru! I knew you were the right person for the job. And frankly, no one else has your track record with bombing raids against the Kryl. I'll send you details about the briefing as soon as it can be arranged."

"Yessir. How long until I can inform the rest of my squad?"

"Give me a few days to get the plan finalized. I'll let you know more when I know more. Until then... start preparing."

"Hard to prepare my squad when I can't tell them what we're doing, sir."

"You're a smart leader, you'll figure it out."

As a matter of fact, she did have training exercises they could run. A few of her pilots had a tendency to break formation when the fighting began, as she'd seen on Yuzosix. Perhaps she could work on that in the meantime.

"Thank you, sir. I won't let the Empire down."

He nodded. Kira turned to go. Her hand was on the doorknob when Ballerdice said, "One more thing, Major. Captain Ruidiaz volunteered to be a test pilot for another, unrelated project."

Her blood went cold. *What? Why didn't Omar tell me that?*

Had he even known? The idea of being separated so suddenly made her feel cold and shivery all over.

All she could say was, "Sir?"

"Something the Ministry of Xeno Affairs has been experimenting with. The extra duty means he won't be part of this mission, however. As his *commander*, I just wanted you to be aware."

"Why wasn't I informed?"

"You're being informed now. Ruidiaz will remain part of the 5th Fighter Wing, but he'll report directly to me for the foreseeable future."

She did her best to keep her tone neutral. "As you wish, sir."

He disarmed the privacy screen by tapping on the clear glass slate of his tab, then pulled up a list of supply shipments and began to study them intently.

She glanced back at him once, then left the office without another word.

FOUR

She found Omar where he'd been every free moment since the Yuzosix mission ended: Bent over an aleacc table, shaking a fistful of dice, and praying to Lady Luck.

She stepped up beside him and whispered, "You owe me an explanation."

He turned his head toward her, eyes sliding from his cup where it lay half-cocked over a pair of dice on the high table. His trademark grin, a roguish smirk full of pearly white teeth, faltered slightly.

It was the same smile that had first melted her heart. Kira hardened herself against a repeat performance. He'd betrayed her trust by not talking to her first. Not only was she his commander, but they were… they were… romantically involved? Dating? Together? No… She didn't know *what* they were, exactly. But it hurt.

So consumed was Kira with this complex mix of emotions warring within that it took her a moment to notice several players around the table staring at them.

She returned Omar's smile with an expression that she

hoped seemed relaxed and carefree to the others. "It can wait until after you lose this hand. I'm in no rush."

He threw his head back and shook with laughter. Omar's mirth drew people's attention in the crowded bar. Smirks and not a few wary looks of concern sprouted around the dice table.

"Thanks for your vote of confidence, Boss," Omar's almond-colored eyes lingered on hers only a moment before turning back to the table. "OK, Stan. I see your five thousand credits, and raise you another ten."

Players groaned. One woman put her head in her hands, and three to Omar's left scooped their dice into their canopies—the name pilots used to refer to the shallow cups concealing their hands.

Kira couldn't help but chuckle to herself.

A0leacc was a game of skill and chance. Some pilots swore the adrenaline rush it gave them was second only to the feel of a plasma drive at full burn.

Each player had their own pair of dice, which they rolled and kept private at the start of a hand. Once rolled, they couldn't be touched. Currently, in this game, four additional dice stood upright in the octagon, a shape at the table's center made of thin black lines.

The job of the players was to use their two dice—their hand, or "hole dice"—plus any three dice dealt inside the octagon (the "community dice"), to form a hand.

Some people called the community dice "the flop," after an ancient Earth game from which this gambling pastime had evolved. Most called it "the octagon" after the shape drawn on the table, and its invisible energy fence.

The dice themselves were twenty-sided. Once activated, they colored into four suits: black, clear, red and blue. The number a die landed on was the number facing up, which was why they had to cover their hands with a cup, or canopy, in order to keep them private.

Right now, there were four transparent (or "white") dice dealt in the octagon. Their numbers were 2, 16, 17, and 18.

Only five dice were dealt into the octagon in each hand, so this was the last roll. And Omar was all out of credits.

"In other words," he said, "I'm all in."

The Oltani holding the dealer's cup gave him a flat look. Only the two of them hadn't folded after Omar raised.

"What are you waiting for, Stan? Come on, baby, gimme that go juice!"

He shrugged. "Your funeral. I call." Stan flung out his hand and a gunmetal-colored die rolled into the center of the table. As it entered the octagon, the die snapped to transparent and a cheer erupted from the onlooking crowd.

The die then struck one of the other dice, and the two bounced off the invisible barrier on the opposite side.

The many cheers turned to strangulated groans as the two dice tumbled end over end and came to rest together —*both* on the number eighteen.

All white: 2, 16, 18, 18, and 20.

Stunned silence spread out into the room from their table. Somewhere, Kira imagined, Lady Luck gloated.

This was an incredible demonstration of the luck factor in aleacc. Once the dice were in the middle of the table, their color had been cast. But if one die got knocked around by another during a roll, its number could *change*—and often did.

The crowd hushed and leaned in sharply as they waited for the final reveal.

Omar pulled his canopy aside with a flourish, revealing a pair of white 18s. "Four of a kind!"

Stan picked up his cup and leered at Omar. "Sorry, not this time, Lima Delta." The joke, slang for 'limp dick,' elicited a round of chuckles. Omar was not amused. His eyes were fixed on Stan's hole dice.

A white 17, and a white 19.

"Straight flush," Stan said.

Omar closed his eyes and rocked back on his heels. His Adam's apple bobbed beneath a three-day growth of black stubble as he swallowed his defeat.

Kira had a moment to take pity on him.

Her patience was quickly overtaken by her anger. She cleared her throat.

"All right, all right." Omar peeled himself from the table and followed her past the bar. "Where are you going?"

"We can't talk here."

She led him out of the rec center to a storage warehouse across the street dedicated to supplying the 4th and 5th Fighter Wings, both stationed here on base in Ariadne's eponymous capital. As a squadron commander, Kira had been granted 24-hour access to grab any standard supplies her squadron needed. Basics like field rations, flight suits, bot repair kits, survival multi-tools. Basically, any dry good they might need on a mission.

Blasters and explosives were kept in another facility that was more tightly controlled.

She also knew that, although security recorded video footage of the supply room, they didn't record the audio. And there was a nice blind spot in the corner by the back door where they could talk without being observed.

When they reached that spot, Kira finally quit moving and turned to face Omar.

"You seem upset," he said.

"I *am*. Why didn't you tell me you were going to be volunteering as a test pilot?"

"You've known for a long time that's what I wanted to do."

"Well, yeah, but I didn't know you had *already made the decision!* You should have told me."

"Sorry, I just got the news this morning. I hadn't seen you yet, so we didn't have a chance to talk."

"You could have come to find me. Instead, you went straight to the aleacc table."

"Sorry, Kit, I told Stan I would be there today. Kind of wish I hadn't, though, after that hand, so point to you."

Kira gestured with her hands, grasping at air and finding no ledge to hang onto. "And don't you think it would have been wise to talk to your squadron commander before making a decision that was going to affect the whole squadron?"

"Aw, come on, Reaper, they like me but I ain't so big-headed as to think y'all can't function without me from time to time."

"What about me? What if *I* need you?"

"Kira." He reached up and rested his hand on her cheek. "I'm not going anywhere, all right?"

She pushed his hand away. "Stop it."

He glanced up at the corner, where a dim red light reminded viewers they were under observation. He sighed.

"I'm sorry, okay? It won't happen again."

She crossed her arms and shifted closer to a large shelf laden with storage bins. "I know *you're* not going anywhere, but the rest of us are."

"What? Where?"

She pressed her lips together and bit her cheek.

He frowned. "What aren't you telling me?"

"The Banshees have been assigned our next mission. It's top secret. I promised Ballerdice I wouldn't share the details yet."

"Come on, honey, it's me."

"*Especially* not you. He *knew*, Omar."

"Knew what?"

Kira glared at him.

"Oh. I see."

"Have you checked your orders?"

"Not in the last few hours…" He dug his tab out of his pocket and called up a hologram interface of his work messages. Resting the slab in his palm, his eyes darted side to side as he scanned through messages. Then his face darkened as he realized what had transpired.

"He can't do that. It wasn't part of the deal."

"What deal?"

"The test pilot program. Ballerdice said it was just extra duty, and promised I wasn't going to be restationed."

She turned the hologram toward her with a gesture and read the orders. "You're not being restationed. It says here you're still based on Ariadne in the 5th Fighter Wing. You just won't be reporting to *me* anymore, but directly to Ballerdice instead. Which means you're off this mission."

"What! No. The test pilot stuff is just *extra* duty. He didn't say anything about cutting me from the squad!"

"Full-time commitment is required for this mission," Kira read from the assignment message.

It was so clear what had happened now. Kira had been completely oblivious to the conniving colonel's maneuvers until it was too late. He'd convinced Omar nothing would change, then yanked the rug out from under them both.

Earth damn you, Ballerdice!

Yet, a part of her hesitated. Would Kira have done anything differently if she were in the wing commander's position? She probably would have been *kinder* about it, speaking to both parties involved before making such a decision, given the sensitive nature of such relationships. But… no, she realized. She would have separated a couple if one was promoted into a position of command over the other. It was too much to risk their behavior compromising a situation where clear thinking and the ability to make rapid decisions saves lives.

She told Omar as much.

"Even so," he said, "this changes nothing between us."

"It does though."

"It doesn't have to. We're good together. We *work*." He reached out and twined her fingers in his. She let him, this time, but kept her hand low and pulled him behind the shelf, bringing him closer.

"We do work," she said. "So, maybe this is for the best. We can still see each other between missions. And now we don't have to be so secretive."

His mind quickly ran the calculations. "But that could mean *months* apart!"

"Other pilots do it. Jim and Felicia Griffin have been married since the second year of the war and they serve in different units."

He growled in his throat.

"Oh, stop it. You'll be *fine*."

"I don't want to be away from you for that long."

"We'll speak over the ansible. We'll write each other every day."

He blew out a heavy breath. "I'll go back to Ballerdice and tell him I've changed my mind."

"No. No, you won't. He did this to separate us. If you make his life difficult, he'll make ours a living hell."

Someone opened the front door to the building. Voices echoed into the warehouse area. They didn't have a line of sight on the newcomers yet, but it was time to go.

"I don't care." Omar wrapped his arm around her waist and pulled her against him. "He can't do this."

"Omar, he already did. It's done."

"That bastard."

She inhaled the pine forest scent of his soap, mingled with an overtone of minty tabac and whisky.

"Watch it!" shouted a man in a loud, brash voice that she recognized. "Who taught you how to drive? You know what, just leave the maglev cart, we'll take it the rest of the way ourselves."

"No problem, sir. Just need you to sign here, please."

After a moment of quiet, a door closed in the distance.

"Why am I surrounded by incompetent people? Hardwell, push this."

"Aye, sir. " That was his adjutant's voice. Lieutenant Hardwell.

"Out!" Kira hissed. "Quickly. Go. Go!"

Omar slipped out the back, and Kira went with him. She eased the door shut, careful to silence the latch, as Ballerdice and his adjutant pushed a maglev cart into the warehouse. They consulted shipping manifests on their tabs, then located an empty shelf and rolled over a ladder.

Omar tugged on her arm. They fled like two sneaking teenagers, giggling at the rush.

Yet she couldn't shake the feeling that she'd lost this hand. In her dealings with the conniving wing commander, she was playing aleacc blind against an opponent throwing weighted dice.

FIVE

The two lovers spent the weekend locked in a top-floor penthouse suite Omar booked for them, *thoroughly* enjoying each other's company.

Although Omar had asked for details, after some consideration, Kira decided to keep the full parameters of her next mission to herself—for now. She insisted Omar be circumspect about the test pilot program, too. He agreed, almost too readily, which made her suspicious, but since it was her idea she couldn't object.

"I've already decided that I'm coming back to the Banshees when my work is done," Omar said.

"You can try," Kira said. "Although it'll take some serious convincing to move Ballerdice. But isn't being a test pilot what you've always wanted?"

"It is… Yeah. I guess it just happened differently than I expected. But yeah, of course I want to do it. You know, there are only a handful of test pilots in the whole Fleet? The best of the best. I've talked to a couple guys and they tell me they're already testing the next generation of starfighters on long-range, hyperspace flights. Can you imagine? Our Scimitars are incredible flying machines, but until they have full hyperspace capability they're not truly versatile enough to deal with the Kryl."

"What are they calling the new models?"

"Sabres."

As he spoke, Kira admired the line of his jaw, the lean cut of his bare shoulder resting on the pillow. Nothing made her happier than witnessing the passion he had for his work. He radiated enthusiasm—and not the empty kind, either. His enthusiasm was backed by years of battle-hardened experience. His confidence and skill in the cockpit made entire flights—entire *squadrons*—rise to his level to compete. Like flying close to a star, they never could approach him as an equal. Yet his very presence seemed to have an uplifting effect on everyone around him.

It was a real shame to lose a pilot like Omar. She almost felt guilty about it. The Fleet desperately needed more good starfighter pilots because not even their extensive recruiting program and a refugee population almost unanimously aligned against the Kryl could keep up with demand. They'd lost too many in the war.

But on the other hand... right now she had Omar all to herself.

The briefing was called for first thing Monday morning.

Colonel Ballerdice stood at the front of the room, nodding quietly while conferring with Rear Admiral Gitano, a short, sober-faced woman with glowing, midnight-dark skin.

Ballerdice studied the room while the woman spoke to him in a hushed voice. The more she talked, the more he looked like he was sucking on a sour urmelon someone mistakenly cut open before it had fully ripened.

"Eh, Gyro… what's up his butt today?" Kira asked her friend.

The wiry bomb squadron commander—real name, Major George Gyrsell—snapped a toothpick between his molars. He leaned over and spat the splintered remains into a trash can. "Hell if I know. I'm a mushroom, Reaper."

By which he meant, kept in the dark and fed shit. A common refrain among soldiers and mid-level officers like the two of them.

"You mean, you don't know?" she asked.

"Do you? The invite for this briefing was about as clear as a fog bank."

"I only know a little bit."

"Well, come on then, quit holding out on me."

She shrugged. They were here now and all would be made clear soon enough. "It's a strike mission," she whispered. "On Planet K."

He gave a small whistle, produced another toothpick from his pocket, and slipped it between his teeth. He glared around at the room as the rest of their flight leads and seconds-in-command wandered in. The briefing would be limited to squadron commanders and those who reported directly to them. It seemed to Kira that Ballerdice was being too careful and overly secretive. What was the danger, really, in briefing the whole team at once? It was more efficient that way, and a good commander was honest with their troops. It's not like word of the mission would leak back to the Kryl…

Then she remembered the ass-chewing Ballerdice got from the minister the other day. Perhaps the real threat to this mission didn't come from the xenos.

As if in response to her thoughts, Lieutenant Hardwell

shut the door to the briefing room. Ballerdice then used his tab to activate an electronic privacy screen. Kira's tab disconnected from the net as it went up.

"Listen up, jockstraps!" he barked. "Nothing we say in here leaves this room. Copy that?"

Sleepy nods and sarcastic mutters of "aye aye, sir" echoed from the audience. Pilots slumped in their seats, exchanged whispered jokes, and cast sardonic glances at the wing commander.

Colonel Ballerdice was not amused.

"I said, do you understand me?" The angry colonel spoke in a scary, quiet voice. As a group, the pilots keyed fully into his mood and realized that they didn't want to be on the receiving end of his ire.

"Yes, sir!" they said, more clearly this time.

"Good. No more whispered jokes or smartass remarks. Admiral Gitano is going to tell you why we're here, and then after she leaves we're going to spend the rest of the morning together poring over the details. Sir, the floor is yours."

Someone chuckled softly at the back of the room. Ballerdice's face darkened to a deep burnished red as he glared, livid. The woman who had giggled—one of Gyro's navigators—strangled the noise in her throat.

Unfazed, the dark-skinned admiral clasped her hands behind her back and stepped forward.

"Thank you, Colonel," she said in a slightly accented voice. Oltanin, maybe? "Welcome to Operation Heartstrike. As you are all no doubt aware, we've bombed the Kryl out of three Solaran colonies, doing so at great cost to the Empire. Not only in terms of lives lost, but also materials, arable farmland, mining operations, and homes for millions of citizens.

"The Fleet does not wish to repeat the experience. Ever. We have lost too much. Millions of our people have been killed, millions more become refugees, and the Colonization Board predicts that we'll be in a housing and food crisis for years to come. Simply put, we cannot *afford* to keep following the same strategy.

"So in addition to doing everything we can to defend the remaining Solaran worlds, we've gathered you here today—the best bomber and fighter squadrons in the entire Fleet—to imagine a future where we no longer have to."

She let those words ring in the air as the pilots' minds caught up with her line of thinking. Eyes widened and there were a few quiet gasps as the gears clicked into place.

"Your objective," Admiral Gitano said, "is to deliver a direct, fatal strike on the heart of Planet K."

"Operation Heartstrike," Kira muttered as the name clicked into place for her.

Colonel Ballerdice looked smug as he called up a hologram of their target. The room fell into a tense hush as the image of a planet completely coated in that purple-black Kryl growth that so reminded her of a devouring cancer appeared between their two senior leaders.

A Fleet of Kryl spacecraft surrounded the dark planet like a cloud of termites. Trails of the creatures streamed from a dozen small moons. Or that's what she thought at first, until she realized that each of the spheres was attached to the world by a tether—or perhaps umbilical cord was a better description…

Sitting next to her, all humor had gone out of Gyro's face. He chomped nervously on his toothpick. The end that stuck out of his mouth had already been frayed.

"How in the name of Animus are we supposed to get through *that*?" asked a nearby captain.

"The Ministry of Xeno Affairs has managed to reverse engineer some Kryl comms tech, and devised stealth technology that will allow us to get in close without being detected."

"Say we do get in unscathed," Gyro drawled, his voice calmer than his demeanor implied. "How are we going to get back out?"

Nods and murmurs of agreement from many.

"You'll have all the support the Fleet can provide," Ballerdice said. "We make a plan, and we execute it."

That didn't sound very reassuring to her. "What kind of casualty rate are you projecting?"

Ballerdice glanced at the admiral.

"We've had our shipmind AIs run numerous simulations and scenarios," said Admiral Gitano. "Casualty rates among the strike force are projected to be anywhere from 50 to 75 percent."

Murmurs of shock rippled through the room. During most of the war, Fleet command refused to clear any mission with simulated casualty rates higher than 5 percent—a hard cutoff for operations enforced stringently to limit their losses.

But I suppose, Kira thought, *Desperate times call for desperate measures.*

As the conversation grew louder—and Ballerdice's face began to redden like a ripe plum—Kira said, "Hey!"

When no one responded, Gyro loosed a sharp whistle from between two teeth.

Every face in the room turned in their direction.

"Be brave, and take heart." Kira stood, even though her heart hammered in her chest and made speaking difficult. "Isn't it the job of every Fleet pilot to face death on a daily basis? This may be more dangerous than other assignments, yes. You might get killed, yes. But if we don't do it, then who will? Do you want this war to go on forever? Do you want the xenos to raze yet another colony?" She raised her eyes and looked from Gitano, to Ballerdice, to Gyro sitting next to her. "I don't like these odds any more than you do. But it's our duty to face danger so that others don't have to. Now, who's with me?"

Gyro's teeth clamped down on the decimated toothpick and his eyes flashed. "I am."

Others called up around the room, and soon they were all hooting and hollering like a pack of excited school children.

The fear didn't go away, but they did manage to shout it into a corner. Kira was still terrified of flying into the hornet's nest. But the feeling was overshadowed by a sense of boldness that came from facing danger head on and *refusing* to back down.

Some called that courage. Some called it duty.

Kira called it giving the middle finger to the xenos who had made their lives a living hell.

Still, in her secret heart of hearts, knowing the danger, she kept one shameful confession to herself: Kira was immensely, intensely relieved that Omar wouldn't be going with them. She didn't know if she could go through with it otherwise.

It was one thing to risk her own life and the lives of her pilots. It was another to risk Omar, the greatest joy she had ever known.

As Ballerdice took over the briefing and began running through logistical details, that shame burrowed deep, and curled up to sleep.

SIX

After the briefing, Kira's squadron flew up to the Fleet's main shipyards in synchronous orbit over Ariadne's capital city and began to train.

"Just six weeks to get in fighting shape," Kira reminded her handpicked team of pilots. "Six weeks before the mission to end all missions."

In hindsight, it made sense why only the commanders had attended the initial briefing with Ballerdice and Gitano: Not all of the pilots in her squadron had been chosen for the top secret assignment.

As with any squadron, the Banshees were a mix of novice and veteran pilots with a range of different qualities. Altogether, they were a force to be reckoned with. But even as decorated as her squadron was, every team had weak links. It took flight time and battle experience for a pilot to develop the cold-blooded steadiness and killer instinct that ensured not just survival, but continual excellence during months-long rotations on the front, flying against the xeno swarm.

So, she'd been forced to cut.

The twenty-four who remained formed a tight-knit, elite

fighting force. Among the top, most battle-tested Scimitar pilots in the Fleet—both in her estimation and in their battle records. It was clear why her squad had been chosen. They were the best of the best.

The same held true for Gyro's bombers. In the end, between the two squads, there were forty-eight personnel total. Each bomber was manned by three people, whereas a Scimitar was a single-person craft. Eight bombers, and twenty-four fighters to alter the course of the war.

No pressure.

Gitano and Ballerdice assured her their combined power would be small enough to slip inside the Kryl's homeworld defense system… and that they'd be carrying a payload large enough to cause massive damage.

This wasn't like the other missions she'd been on, where hundreds or even thousands of starships would be deployed against critical Kryl defenses, structures, or forces. Stealth was the name of the game.

Those who were cut from the team were separated off. The starfighters went on a refugee escort mission, while the bombers and navigators were sent to the front to support another squadron.

The forty-eight pilots left began the most grueling training course of their lives—made harder by the presence of everyone's favorite wing commander. "Come on, Phoenix!" he shouted at one of her pilots during a training drill. "Get your head out of your ass and into the game!"

If you asked Kira, Ballerdice was *too* involved, though she wouldn't dream of voicing complaint.

The wing commander had flown to orbit with them and conducted his work from an office he commandeered there. He was currently watching the starfighter flights take turns on the obstacle course from the warmth and comfort of the observation tower.

Kira could see him gesturing and shouting behind the glass from where she sat in her Scimitar in a stationary parked position near the metal gate marking the course's finish line.

"Lower, Razorback! Earth dammit, are you slow or just stupid?"

She gritted her teeth. Kira hated when other people insulted her pilots. It was one thing if she did it—joking around, giving each other a hard time, it was all part of the camaraderie that held a team together. But she didn't see the point of leading through fear and intimidation like Ballerdice seemed to like doing.

Razorback's Scimitar curled around a corner and came into the final run, a narrow tunnel made of adjustable metal struts that crossed at the top and would funnel his ship lower and lower as he sped into the final gate.

"That's it, Razorback," she said. "Hug the floor."

He was flying good, straight and low, as he got deeper into the tunnel. Kira could hear him breathing deeply over the squad-wide broadband. Then an autonomous probe suddenly activated and darted in front of him.

Razorback inhaled sharply as he was forced to rotate to avoid contact.

His left wing struck the probe, sending it ricocheting off two different struts before denting his aluminite canopy in the aft portion. That startled him, causing the man to twitch on his throttle, and suddenly his Scimitar's belly was dragging a big red mark along the "floor" as his ship came into contact with the protective energy shield positioned around the lower struts of the tunnel. His starfighter wobbled as he fought to regain control.

A horn sounded in Kira's audio feed that indicated a course failure. "You're dead, Razorback."

"Son of a bitch!" he snarled as he skated across the finish

line and pulled out of contact with the energy shield. "Where'd that bloody probe come from?"

"We've got to be ready for anything. If a little probe scares you here, what will you do if you get surprised by a Kryl gunship at close range?"

Ballerdice sneered, spun on his heel and marched back into the space station. "Amateurs, the lot of you," he muttered. "You've got your work cut out for you, Miyaru. Only five weeks left. Don't screw this up."

Kira's resolve hardened. She ignored her commander's remark, being sure to keep the annoyance out of her tone as she gave her squadron new orders over broadbeam. "Razorback, dock your ship for repair and refuel. Eclipse, you're up next in the tunnel. In the meantime, we're drilling escort formations. Goldie, Gunner, Fang and Silverfox, you've got Bomber Four…"

She keyed a few buttons and a far away portion of the obstacle course twisted and danced through space, reconfiguring into something that resembled the surface of the mountainous, ice-covered approach along Planet K's north pole. They planned to go in that way, flying for a thousand klicks a few hundred feet above the ground to avoid radar detection on their way to the Queen Mother's lair—their ultimate target.

Despite Ballerdice's inspirational presence and motivational tone—*cue eye roll*, she thought—the training course drills moved along at a fast clip. Her pilots made mistakes, of course. They were the best, but they were still human no matter how much the Fleet's AI flight support systems and stimchem helped improve their reaction times and movements. By the third week, however, they were all so familiar with the landscape, formations, flight patterns, and Kryl surface-to-air defensive turrets that they could fly the mission in their sleep.

Many of them did. With training this intense, flying dreams were common.

And, often, flying nightmares.

The only thing she couldn't prepare for, of course, was the unknown. All she could do, all any pilot could do, was pour their heart and soul into training, and trust their instincts to bring them home safe.

They wouldn't all make it back. Kira was starting to accept this uncomfortable truth, and it seemed like everyone felt the pressure and imminent danger such knowledge imparted.

Fear hung in the pauses between tactical conversations in the briefing room. It lingered in the shadowed corners of their quarters. It waited behind the closed eyelids of every person. More than one pilot had reported waking in a cold sweat, fists gripped tightly on an imaginary throttle while the Kryl hive queen's insectoid laughter echoed in the distance— a sound no living human had ever heard, but which all imagined as the stuff of nightmares.

In the fourth week, they returned to the ground base on Ariadne for a day of rest followed by a transfer to the jungle for survival training. No one under her command thought they'd survive if they crash landed on Planet K, but the Ministry of Xeno Affairs' planetary climatologists assured them the atmosphere was breathable, so they would have to do the training.

It wasn't the atmosphere that worried Kira. But orders were orders. Off to survival training they went.

Omar was waiting for her on the tarmac when she landed for their rest day. Kira popped her canopy and hopped out. Her boots struck the ground, and she matched his big smile.

"Good to see you, Boss."

"Hey, sugar. Good to see you, too. But I ain't your boss anymore, remember?"

"Actually," he said, "I have some good news. I put in for a transfer. I'm coming back to the squad!"

Her gut twisted as if two strong hands had reached into her belly and made fists.

"What? Why?"

"I got wind of what you're cooking up. Planet K? Sounds like a mission I don't want to miss."

She growled angrily as her stomach churned. It was no surprise that someone had given him the juicy details. He was part of the team and carried a lot of influence with the other pilots. Only a matter of time before someone caved under the pressure of his questioning. Kira was surprised she'd held out for so long.

"Besides," he said, "I don't think this test pilot thing is for me."

"But Omar, you've just barely gotten started."

"And already I know I'd rather be on a fighter squad than flying experimental spacecraft for some MOXA goons."

"But why?"

"Those ships don't even work right."

"Yeah. 'Experimental,' remember?"

"It's…" He shuddered. Like actually, physically, shook. "Well, it's not pleasant, let's just leave it at that. Besides, I don't even get to shoot anything. I'm missing all the fun!"

She couldn't help but chuckle. However, Kira could tell he wasn't sharing the whole truth. "It's not like you to give up so easily. What's really going on?"

The rest of the pilots were in the process of taxiing into their parking spots in the hangar. Ballerdice, who had flown ahead with a cargo plane, was out on the tarmac overseeing the unloading of some cargo he'd retrieved in orbit, generic supply crates used to rotate dead batteries and broken bot parts back from the station for repair or recycle. For whatever reason, Colonel Ballerdice was pacing around the unloading ramp, barking orders and criticizing their technique.

"Omar?" she said when he didn't answer.

"Hm?" Instead of responding to her question, he studied their wing commander with narrowed eyes.

"What's going on with you?" Kira asked again.

"Ballerdice is acting weird. What's a wing commander doing breathing down the neck of that loadmaster?"

"What's that got to do with you quitting as a test pilot?"

"Nothing." He turned back to face her. Kira longed to reach out to him, to hold him in her arms, but the other pilots were unloading now and it wouldn't be seemly to display that kind of affection in front of her crew.

He must have had the same thought, because Omar reached out and brushed her arm with his fingers. She took half a step back and he let his hand drop.

"Are you mad at Ballerdice for reassigning you?"

"He's such an asshole."

"Well, yeah. What else is new?"

As he said it, Ballerdice leaned forward to whisper-shout another demand into the ear of the Spacecraft Loadmaster. Veins popped in the man's neck, but he gritted his teeth and paced away instead of exploding at the colonel.

"How does someone like that get to be in charge, anyway?" Omar asked.

"Earth knows. But he's just a distraction, Omar. Think about your own future."

His eyes darkened. "I have. I'll go talk to Ballerdice if he doesn't approve my transfer soon." He gave her a crooked half-smile. "Just wanted you to hear it from me, Boss."

The vice around her guts tightened, causing her stomach to spasm.

It wasn't just that Omar was unhappy, or that it seemed like he was giving up on a lifelong dream without putting in the effort to make it work.

It was that rejoining her squad meant he would be sent into danger with the rest of them. No way they would leave a pilot as talented as Ruidiaz behind.

Just when she thought his neck would be spared the noose, he shoved his ignorant head right back in.

SEVEN

"What is it, Major?" Colonel Ballerdice asked without looking up.

Kira snapped her heels together and fired off a sharp salute. "Thank you, sir, for fitting me into your busy schedule."

She needed him to be in an agreeable mood. It had been a pain in the neck to get an appointment, but complaining would get her nowhere.

"Hngh," Ballerdice grunted from between two holo-screens—one full of logistics spreadsheets, the other displaying a calendar so packed you'd think he was campaigning for Busybody of the Year in the military pencil pusher category.

She fought to keep any trace of the disdain she felt from showing on her face. "Sir, I came to make a small request."

"Survival gear outfittings are standardized Fleet-wide, so I can't add any extra provisions to your troop's kit without submitting a separate budget request form."

"Of course, sir. But we have more than we need for the

upcoming training. Plus, a few extra items provisioned especially for this mission."

He perked up. "By who?"

When it came to a good mystery, Ballerdice was like a ship rat catching scent of the fermentation tanks.

"Ministry of Xeno Affairs."

His eyes widened and then he pretended not to care. But she'd caught the glint of eagerness in his eyes. He wanted to know more.

"Good gear?" Ballerdice feigned disinterest, studying his holoscreens.

"Top quality oxygen tanks and gillbreathers, for one. A couple danger detection bots."

"Huh. Well, good. Those MOXA guys know more than anyone else about the terrestrial environment on Planet K."

"Yessir."

"So what can I do for you, Major?"

The words she'd rehearsed on the way over squirmed and hid under her tongue for a moment. She forced them out. "Sir, is it true that Captain Ruidiaz put in for a transfer back to the Banshees?"

He studied her carefully. "It is."

"I'd like you to deny his request."

As soon as the words exited her mouth, her limbs went weak and shaky. Her heart hammered in her chest.

"Is that so?"

"Yes. That is, if you agree, sir."

"How interesting." Ballerdice cocked his head. The man may have been insufferable, but he wasn't stupid. "You're trying to keep your man out of danger, aren't you?"

"My man?" she asked, caught off guard.

"Your pilot." Ballerdice smirked. He was taunting her.

"No, sir," she lied, maintaining a neutral expression though it felt like her face was burning up. "It's just... I've been flying at Ruidiaz's side for years. He's always tried to push boundaries. Go faster, fly farther, break records. He's a great fighter, don't get me wrong, and we're worse off without him. But he was *born* to be a test pilot. He'll be brilliant at it. Maybe one of the best we've ever had."

"I don't disagree with that sentiment. It's an astute observation. And it's honorable that you would willingly forego an advantage like Ruidiaz on the upcoming mission because you want the best for your pilot—and for the Fleet."

"I do," Kira said, feeling some relief to find that she meant it.

"Very well," the colonel said, returning his attention to the holoscreens. He made a gesture that transformed the data into a complex graph full of lines and semi-translucent shapes. Tracking data on shipments coming and going through the Fleet's main spaceport and their various supply depots, she thought, although she couldn't be certain. It was hard to focus on the specifics when seen in reverse with privacy blurring activated.

Kira stood at attention for several long seconds.

"Is there something else, Major?"

"No, sir. Uh, just so I'm clear, you'll do it?"

"In point of fact, I had already decided to deny the captain's transfer request. Now, I have yet another reason to do so. If you don't mind, I've got a packed schedule and no time to waste. Never know when another *surprise* appointment will pop up." He glanced at her, his brows furrowed in irritation.

"Thank you, sir." She fled before he could change his mind.

The bounce was back in her step. She could focus, once again, on the mission.

EIGHT

To Kira's consternation, even though his transfer request had been denied, Omar and several other test pilots were sent alongside the Banshees to their week of survival training.

And Earth knew why, but Ballerdice came, too. "Annual refresher courses are required for every Fleet officer to stay battle certified," he droned on in the transport shuttle. "And this year's course is doubly important since MOXA is switching up your kits to better equip pilots who find themselves in Kryl-occupied territory."

The wing commander seated himself beside her on their passenger flight out, forcing her to keep any candid conversation with Omar to a minimum. Frustrated at the situation and bored from hours in transit, Kira allowed herself a rare moment of candidness with her wing commander. "I don't know why we bother, sir. If you look at the stats, the vast majority of pilots killed in action die from direct fire, suffocating in vacuum, or being destroyed upon impact. Only a fraction of those—less than one percent!—put boots on the ground in survival situations."

"And of those that do," Gyro added, leaning in from where he sat across the aisle, "only a handful make it out alive."

"So what are we doing here, sir?" Kira asked. "With all due respect, it's a waste of time. This is an aerial mission. If I'm on the ground, I've already failed. Besides, there's no extraction from Planet K, and you know it."

He grunted. Shrugged. "Chalk it up to SOPs. Protocol. It's the same training the Marines get. Nothing I can do about it. I talked to MOXA and they just want to make sure we're as prepared as we can be."

Gyro rolled his eyes—subtly, when Ballerdice was looking the other way. Kira fell into a brooding silence for the rest of the flight.

Another squadron was rotating back as her people unloaded into a compound nested deep in a tropical jungle on the opposite side of Ariadne. By the time they started hitching their packs up and setting off for their week in the wilderness, another squad was already rolling in behind them.

Too much training, too little time.

The further into the jungle they went, the swampier the ground got. Soon her whole body, her blaster, and every piece of equipment was coated in a thick layer of moisture and muck. It was the closest thing to simulating a Kryl environment they had. If you closed your eyes and imagined that, laced through humidity so thick you could cut it with a knife, noxious fumes also emanated from vents in the ground while radioactive sulfur ponds dotted vast swathes of lowland, and burrows in the rising hills led deep into the Kryls' underground lairs, it was just like being on an alien world.

The Ministry of Xeno Affairs, or MOXA, had provided briefings on all the new tech, especially the gillbreathers, which were designed to extract the toxic elements from the air as it passed into your mouth. They could also function as second lungs, extending underwater breathing for up to twenty minutes. Incredibly useful if you found yourself surrounded by Kryl and near a body of water, since Kryl tracked by scent and had trouble with water.

Kira hoped to Animus she never found herself in that skin-crawling situation.

Other than that, her week was mostly a familiar experience. Long hikes, rough camping, survival skills training. The course instructors gave lectures on SERE—Survival, Evasion, Resistance and Escape—drilling the procedures into their memory. They conducted several drills where trailing dogs were let loose on groups of pilots while they tried to evade capture.

Annoyingly, only Omar and his test pilot buddies made it cleanly through that drill. They found a shallow pond in a valley and used the gillbreathers to hide underwater.

Exactly like they were supposed to. They were just the only ones with the *stones* to stay underwater as long as it took for the dogs to pass by.

As it turned out, the pond had been filled with a nasty species of algae—and carnivorous fish. The four test pilots spent the night barfing up the contents of their stomach while nursing multiple bite wounds.

They were laughing maniacally and cracking jokes through the whole experience, jealously guarding the bottles of whisky that were their winnings in the contest even though they were in no shape to enjoy it.

"Earth-damned test pilots," muttered Gyro by the fire that night, in his characteristic grouchy manner. "They're all batshit, every one of 'em."

"Ain't that the truth," Kira said.

Omar raised a glass to her from his spot leaning against a

gnarled stump by a ravine. He drank, puked over the edge, then drank again to wash the taste away.

Kira shook her head, bemused, and sipped at her water. "Stubborn idiot," she said fondly.

Kira wasn't drinking that night because she wanted to remain clear-headed. There was too much on her mind, and she couldn't afford to let her focus wander.

Although she was eager to get back to space and continue flight drills that were *actually* relevant to this mission, her squad stayed an extra day to let everyone rest and recover—as well as the test pilots. Most of them, Omar included, stayed inside and played card games.

Kira found she couldn't sit still. She had energy to burn despite having just completed a week of survival training.

It wasn't so much physical energy as a churning anxiety that needed an outlet. She didn't relish the idea of hiking or hitting the gym, not after what they'd just been through. Instead, she took a skimmer bike from the depot and blazed out on curving dirt roads. Headlights illuminated pock-marked trails that zoomed below her hovering vehicle. The roads were lined with overgrown brush that was thick enough to stand on. She zipped and burned away from base, venturing through small villages and rustic, sleepy towns far from the hustle and bustle of the capital planet's urban core.

A cool wind—so rare in this climate—whipped at her face, compressing her cheeks as she zoomed along until finally finding the paved open road. She increased her speed, leaning into each turn, tilting the skimmer at steep angles as she hugged the curving white lines of the road. Kira found a trail into the foothills and decided to climb. Her arms and legs trembling from gripping the handles for so long, she finally coasted into a high overlook, parked the bike and dismounted.

Below, half a dozen small villages dotted the tropical

lowlands. Dim electric lights shone from the jungle, each cluster several kilometers apart. Down in the valley, the villages seemed so remote from each other. But up here she could see how they were all part of the same ecosystem.

It seemed like a peaceful life. Maybe one day, after she retired, Kira and Omar could settle down in a place like this. No thought of war, or the Kryl, or their next mission. Just a small house on a hill with a small garden, maybe a pool...

She shook her head. It was a distant, fanciful dream. She already knew that Omar would be restless in a place so far from casinos and the nightlife of Ariadne's capital. But maybe that could change, given time. He would settle down eventually, wouldn't he?

Gradually, looking out into the night, her heartbeat slowed and her hands stilled. When, at last, she climbed back on the skimmer she thought, *This is what I'm fighting to protect.*

Peace. Home. The right of these villages to exist. The right of these people to sleep in peace, to dream, to build their lives and raise their children somewhere safe.

Somewhere not under threat of alien invasion.

This was why her mission mattered.

With a renewed sense of clarity and purpose, Kira began to make her way back to base. She guided the vehicle more slowly this time, enjoying the soft motion of air rushing beneath her.

She found she didn't need to grip the handles so hard anymore.

As she came out of the final village and into the straightaway that led to the gate of the Fleet compound, something caught her attention in the sky to the east, a blurring shape that moved across the blue-tinged face of the moon.

She came to an intersection and turned toward the movement. The road meandered slightly before branching off into a copse of large trees that gave way to a clearing on the bank of a small river.

That's where she'd seen the blurred shape come down.

As she edged closer, a soft humming noise gave form to her suspicions.

Not just a shape, but a ship—flying under stealth.

Is it one of the experimental starfighters the test pilots have been using? Or something else?

On a hunch, Kira shut off the skimmer and leaned it against a tree trunk. She strode softly forward, trying to stay quiet, until she came to the edge of the treeline, with the clearing and river in view.

A transport marked with the MOXA logo had set down. It was an unbelievably unsexy ship—nothing more than a large cube with curved walls. A small cargo ship.

Nearby a truck had been parked. Its tailgate was propped open and a few supply crates had been slid into the bed. Ballerdice stood by the tailgate, bathed in moonlight with his back to her. He was speaking to a man in a gray ministry uniform whose eyes darted nervously around while Ballerdice was speaking. The wing commander had that effect on people.

Or was this something else? Some kind of illicit exchange? The late timing and location reeked of suspicion. Was this why Ballerdice insisted on coming to survival training with them?

And what in all the livable worlds did MOXA have that Ballerdice wanted?

Ballerdice closed the tailgate of the truck and opened the door.

Before she could be noticed, Kira sneaked away, hopped back on her skimmer bike, and sped home to base.

She didn't know what Ballerdice was up to, but getting involved would be a bad idea. If she was wrong about what she saw, Colonel Ballerdice would rain hell down on her for accusing him of wrongdoing based on circumstantial evidence. He'd be up her ass the rest of this mission. Or worse, remove her from it, leaving an ominous strike on her record.

No, she couldn't risk getting involved. For all she knew, the wing commander had good reasons for arranging surreptitious supply dropoffs in the middle of the night.

Didn't he?

NINE

Back in orbit, the remaining few weeks of training passed quickly in the way that a dawn-till-midnight, breakneck schedule sometimes does.

The days were long, but training was over in the blink of an eye.

In the end, Kira rested satisfied that she'd given it her full effort.

No regrets.

She didn't have as much time to spend with Omar during all of this as she usually did, but since he was doing training in space—at an unnamed location in Ariadne's solar system, where test pilots could work on their experimental spacecraft in secret—he still came back to base to sneak into her room one or two nights per week.

When they got together, both were inevitably exhausted, but most of the time they didn't sleep right away. They would make love slowly and snuggle close in the afterglow. They talked about deep things like their future together, and where they might live. About their childhoods and whether or not they wanted kids of their own.

It felt good to imagine the possibilities. It gave her hope.

It gave her life.

"I'm going to come back, Omar," Kira said, finally voicing the unspoken dark cloud that sometimes settled between them.

"I know you are," he said. "I just wish I could go with you."

I don't, she thought. "It's better this way. Only one of us has to risk our lives."

"I wish it were me."

"Don't say that. I signed up for this. It's my duty to see it through."

"It's what I signed up for, too, remember?"

"Sometimes life sends us down an unexpected path."

"I just wish there was another way…"

Wishing she hadn't opened her stupid mouth, Kira kissed him to shut him up. They made love for a second time that night and fell into an exhausted sleep.

She woke once to see Omar lying awake, twirling what looked like an oversized diamond banded with metal in his hand. It sparkled in the starlight leaking in through the porthole windows of her private bunk.

He was gone before she woke the next morning, and she thought what she saw might have been a dream. Maybe it was her subconscious's way of telling herself she wanted to marry him. Why else would she imagine Omar holding a giant, glittering gemstone? He couldn't afford something like that on his salary. Not yet, anyway.

———

Finally, launch day for their mission came.

Her squad had already moved their Scimitars into the bay of the heavy cruiser, a smaller ship than the destroyer on which they were usually stationed because a smaller ship would be less likely to be detected by the Kryl.

They also didn't want to alert the Kryl that any sort of special mission was being launched. This ship and another carrying the bombers would depart separately, moving in two different directions, and then rendezvous just out of range of Planet K for the final approach.

"The Fleet is moving into position now," Colonel Ballerdice told her on the bridge of the heavy cruiser. He'd shipped out with them, toting his adjutant and leaving his second-in-command in charge of the wing. "By the time we get there, the bulk of the Kryl swarm should be off defending their new mining operations, leaving us an opening to slip in undetected."

"How thoroughly have they tested the stealth tech that's supposed to disguise us?"

"I already told you, we used it to perform reconnaissance on Yuzosix before the last attack."

She sucked air through her teeth and shook her head. "I don't trust it. Their home planet is a different environment. Planet K is much more developed, which makes me think it's likely their early-detection capabilities are more advanced in their home territory."

"MOXA didn't give me any reason to think that was the case."

"They don't know everything."

Colonel Ballerdice grunted. "You're not wrong about that."

"So it's possible the stealth tech won't work."

He glanced at her, but said nothing. That was as much admission as she was likely to get.

I have to tell Gyro, Kira thought. *He needs to know.*

He already suspected. They'd practiced evasive maneuvers for the approach countless times during their weeks of training. She would simply tell him to be ready to execute those. No pilot liked surprises and it was more realistic to expect shit to go sideways than to close your eyes, cross your fingers, and hope the mission proceeded without a hitch.

A lurching motion caught her off-guard as the ship dropped out of hyperspace. It had taken two days of multiple jumps to get here, but that was supposed to be the last one.

The cruiser's captain confirmed as much over the intercom. "We're here, folks. Stay alert. Deploying recon probes now."

Equipped with the same stealth technology her fighters would use, the mechanical probes would give them a camera angle of Planet K at up to a thousand times magnification. In the meantime, the bomber crews were supposed to take a shuttle over here so they could do their final briefing together.

Kira's thoughts were so consumed with the mission that when Captain Omar Ruidiaz walked into the war room wearing his flight suit and his characteristic wild grin, she almost fainted.

"Hey, Boss," he said.

Kira just stared at him in shell-shocked silence.

"I know!" he said. "Surprised me, too. But MOXA decided they wanted me on this mission after all."

And you didn't think to warn me? she thought furiously. But no words would come out.

Her heart slammed against her ribcage and her breath started coming fast. Omar's presence changed everything. Kira's hands clenched and she drove her fingernails into her palms so hard her arms started shaking. She tried to turn away before it turned into a scene, but Omar caught her arm.

"Whoa!" he said. "Boss, what's the matter? You're white as a sheet."

Idiot. "What are you doing here, Omar?"

"I told you, orders. MOXA sent me here to help."

"Why the hell'd they have to go and do that?"

He flinched like she'd just kicked his favorite puppy. Omar licked his lips and held her gaze before breaking, briefly, to glance at Colonel Ballerdice.

Kira turned toward him. Did he have something to do with it?

The wing commander threw up his hands. "Not my decision," he said. "Just following Earth-damned orders. Now, let's get to work. We have an Overmind to incinerate."

"Well, screw me sideways running."

"Gyro!" Kira said, chuckling softly. He made her laugh, and a touch of humor always helped soothe her nerves when she was staring death in the face.

"What? You see that, don'tcha?"

She'd already told him about the likelihood of the stealth tech failing them. Now, a stealth tech malfunction seemed like a minor problem compared to the dreaded sight on the holoscreen at the front of the war room.

Orbital space around Planet K was *packed* with Kryl creatures and starships. Hundreds of thousands of them. Maybe a million. The shipmind AI was still calculating an estimate, and as she got closer to certainty the six figure number continually edged up in the corner of the screen.

"That's a whole freakin' lot of dust-sucking xeno scum to wade through," Kira finally said. "What do we do, Colonel?"

"We wait for Fleet operations to draw them out."

"Weren't they supposed to have done that already?" Omar asked.

Huh, Kira thought. *Someone must have briefed him separately. What else was Ballerdice keeping from her?*

Colonel Ballerdice grunted. "Days ago. While we were in transit."

"Not exactly a short trip here," Kira said. "And combat is unpredictable. We should bunker down and keep our eyes peeled."

"If the diversion don't work to draw 'em out," Gyro said, "seems like we ain't getting through."

"It'll work," Ballerdice said. "Trust me."

To a person, every single officer around her rolled their eyes, clenched their jaw, or otherwise made some expression of contempt for the wing commander's certainty.

It wasn't that Ballerdice hadn't seen battle. Nearly every officer in the Fleet had been in a real firefight.

But pencil pushers like Ballerdice experienced it from a distance. They specialized in impersonal statistics and technically correct tactical decisions.

They didn't fly straight into the arms of the enemy or get close enough to see their slavering jaws and glistening sharp teeth.

TEN

Ballerdice ended up being right. It annoyed her, but Kira wasn't one to hold grudges and she quickly let it go. He may have been a burr in her side, but so what?

She had a job to do.

Besides, she was more concerned with how Omar's presence kept distracting her from the mission.

She was furious at him. Not because he'd been assigned to this mission at the last minute. She was used to capricious command decisions like that.

She was pissed because he hadn't warned her.

He didn't even send an ansible message while they were in transit!

And he had the *nerve* to try to slip into her bunk—a bunk she was sharing with another pilot because her squad had odd numbers—in the middle of the night and get cozy.

She kicked him out.

And when, instead of feeling justified, she felt *disappointed he was gone*, she got mad at herself.

Which made her even angrier because she was wasting precious mental space and energy on their relationship instead of focusing on the mission like she was supposed to be.

"Earth, what is wrong with me?" she demanded, staring into the mirror the next morning.

Her heart held the answer.

You love that idiot.

But she wasn't ready to forgive him for playing loose with the truth.

Fortunately, when the Fleet's diversion finally did work, and half the Kryl forces abruptly departed from the system, she quickly became too busy to worry about it.

The interminable waiting ended, and Kira shoved her complex mix of emotions for Omar into a shadowy corner, to be dealt with at a later date.

Twenty-four hours after the Kryl force departed, her squadron finally deployed.

"Feast your eyes upon the balls," Omar said sardonically over the squad-wide broadbeam channel. "The balls, in all their xeno glory."

Nervous laughter echoed back in response.

Kira's squadron was approaching Planet K and its many satellites. Each one looked like a not-quite-round tennis ball the color of ink, attached at the end of a long string stretching down toward the planet. There were two large moons, as well. But these smaller spheres... they weren't moons. They were undeniably Kryl in nature—alien, insectoid, wrapped in many layers like a spider's nest or a caterpillar's cocoon. Their surface was pockmarked, and glistened purplish-black striations.

Kira double checked her navigation. "You can see the

drones clustered around them. It's like they're a bunch of tiny space stations."

No Kryl had spotted their approach yet. They'd already activated the stealth tech, and they'd be in range within minutes.

"Not exactly," Ballerdice interjected. "According to the MOXA scientists, those there are orbital spawning pools."

She rolled her eyes. What a know-it-all. They'd all gotten the MOXA reports. Did he really think he was the only one who'd read them? "Are you saying they *make babies* there, Colonel?"

The moment the words had left her lips, her eyes widened. *Earthing idiot! Did I really just say that to my wing commander?*

Omar's sarcastic wit was infectious and she'd caught the disease.

"Affirmative," Colonel Ballerdice said, apparently missing the joke entirely. A pause held the line while he listened to a MOXA xenoscientist give a detailed explanation. Then he translated the science mumbo-jumbo to the rest of them: "Apparently, the Overmind spawns the brood in space, and workers gradually expose them to vacuum over time, treating them with chemicals so that their carapaces harden until they become like sealed starship hulls. It takes months for a drone to become fully space-adapted."

"Clever," Omar said.

"And gross," muttered Gyro.

"I'd love to see how space-adapted they are if I put a few holes in their bellies," Omar said.

"That's a distraction, Captain," Ballerdice said. "There are too many and attacking them is the best kind of early warning the Overmind can have. Stay focused on the mission."

Kira found she agreed with him. It helped that Ballerdice

was on his best behavior. Word had it that this mission was now being monitored by Emperor Aeris, the enduring youth himself, sovereign of the Solaran Empire and all her colonies—on the bright side, their wing commander hadn't insulted anyone since they launched from the heavy cruiser.

Kira flipped over to the squad-only broadbeam, an encrypted private channel that cut Ballerdice and other bystanders out of the loop. "If one of those spawning pools happens to be in our way as we exit, it counts as an enemy in my book."

Chuckles and laughter echoed into her helmet's headphones.

"Aye aye, Major Miyaru," Gyro drawled.

"Copy that, Boss," Omar said.

She grinned, then frowned. She wanted to be angry with Omar, but it was so damn good to have him back on the team. His simple presence lifted everyone's spirits. As a result, partly because of him and partly because of the jittery excitement of *finally* being here, morale was high.

Kira hardened her resolve and re-focused. She checked her navigation again.

"All right folks, time to make our first move. Banshees, on me!"

The pathfinding system turned a straight line into a curve on her screen and she nosed forward until she was on a trajectory to intercept Planet K.

The blip on her heads-up display representing her Scimitar crossed the invisible line marking where MOXA believed the Kryl's visual and radar detection capabilities began.

Kira held her breath.

After thirty seconds, she blew it out. No alarm had sounded.

They were in.

<h1 style="text-align:center">ELEVEN</h1>

The stealth tech held, so Kira flew in silence and counted her lucky stars.

There were a few bright specks in the distance, planets in the local system which shone green-blue and red. As the Kryl satellites grew larger in her front window, she wondered if she'd ever see her native stars again, or if she'd die under this alien sky.

Was it macabre to visualize your own death when facing danger? To imagine your destruction in all its gruesome glory? She always thought it was an odd habit, but this was simply how her mind worked. Better to prepare yourself for the possibility and be ready when it came than the other way around.

"Passing checkpoint one," Kira whispered quietly into her comms. MOXA had reassured them that while the broad-beam channel back to Ballerdice could be detected by Kryl, their encrypted private channel—called a "tightbeam"—couldn't be hacked. Still, neither she nor anyone else chattered on comms.

Nerves were too high and it wasn't worth the risk.

Beyond the first checkpoint, they passed within a hundred thousand klicks of the first drone patrols. It got tighter after that. Kryl patrols became more numerous until they were passing within fifty thousand klicks, then twenty, then ten.

In the vast distances of space, passing at five thousand kilometers was practically close enough to high five each other.

Not that the Kryl were into high fives. Their version of a high five involved razor sharp talons and a lot more firepower.

Her heads-up display beeped once. "Second checkpoint complete."

"Look at those things," Omar whispered over the tight-beam, finally breaking the silence. "They're like electrical cables tying each cocoon to the planet."

Kira was close enough now to see one of them in detail with the naked eye. The satellites were a kilometer wide and twice as tall. Each was attached to the planet by a thick tether, or shaft, fifty meters in diameter. The structure was certainly sturdy enough to weather any storms that might pass through the atmosphere below. But how did they build —or grow—something so huge? How did they stabilize a tether stretching into space? Her pilot's mind wondered at the advanced understanding of physics and engineering that must be required to build such structures—and not just one, but dozens spread across the face of the planet.

As she was staring at the one near her, the shaft darkened near the top as some kind of object seemed to pass through it.

She gasped as the realization struck her. Not a tether—but a space elevator! Of course, that must be how the Kryl accessed the pods. She used her HUD's camera to zoom in—and saw legs squirming inside.

Her attention seemed to halt the creature's passing.

It scuttled around in the shaft.

Her HUD beeped frantically.

"Oh, crap," she muttered.

The thing inside plummeted back toward the planet. How it could move so quickly in zero G, she had no idea. Must be some kind of liquid propulsion system.

She didn't have time to follow the thought because Omar shouted, "Incoming fire!"

"Earth," Kira cursed. Had it really seen her through their stealth tech? She *knew* that stuff was unreliable. "Evade and defend!"

Kira smashed her thumbs into the stimchem trigger and shoved her throttle to max burn. The rest of the banshees and Gyro's bombers did the same, moving erratically to avoid taking fire as bolts of plasma raked across their shields.

Kira and a few others pulled ahead of the bombers. Gyro's ships had more mass to move, especially with their payload.

"Ahh, hell, he's on my back, I—"

Sudden silence. Kira glanced at her radar just as one of her Scimitars blinked out of existence.

And so it begins.

"Steady," Kira said. "Get those drones off our tail, Gyro!"

"You got it, Reaper."

Around them, Kryl drones began to converge. A few larger ships pointed roughly toward their location.

Gyro's ships dropped carpet bombs behind them. The explosives spread out and were set to detonate the moment they detected enemy units. Each explosion also expelled chaff that would fuzz the Kryl sensors as they mimicked the radar/lidar reflection of Fleet starcraft, making the enemy think they were more numerous than they actually were, and send them scrambling to defend against a specter squadron that didn't actually exist.

Her HUD beeped. "Third checkpoint!" Kira shouted. "Fire more chaff into the atmosphere, now!"

"They're closin' on us, Reaper," Gyro said.

"We can make it. Take aim and fire!"

Another two starfighters and a bomber blinked off the radar behind her. She aimed her own weapons and fired past the nearest space elevator stretching down from a tethered satellite.

The shot was on target. Her round bloomed in the atmosphere, leaving a shower of chaff that was designed to make the enemy think her Scimitars entered at that location.

In a fit of pique, she also aimed a heat-seeker at the nearest spawning pool. Her projectile hit the target, sinking the top half of the egg like a lung collapsing in on itself.

"Nice shot!" Omar said. "Oh, fu—hang on!"

Kira's heart leapt into her throat and she stared at her HUD, breath held, as she waited to see what happened to Omar.

"Spidermonkey, are you okay?" His ship was still there on her radar. "Pull around and meet us at the north pole."

"There's a pack on my tail! I'll lead them away."

"You're going the wrong direction!"

"Only three left. I've got 'em. You move in and I'll meet you down there."

The idea made her anxious, but what choice did she have? He was the best pilot in her squadron. If anyone could handle three drones on his own, it was Omar.

"Be careful," she said. "Everyone else, with me. Stay tight!"

The rest of their flight into the atmosphere was a harried, frantic experience. Packs of Kryl ships came up from the surface to attack them from all sides. They were surprised by a few and took serious losses, mostly among her starfighter pilots as they fought valiantly to protect Gyro's bombers, who carried the important payloads.

Gyro himself carried one of the Queen-killers, the word they'd taken to using for the burrowing bomb that would dig down and strike at the heart of the Overmind's lair.

To her dismay, Admiral Gitano's initial attrition estimates weren't far off. When they finally entered the stratosphere of Planet K, the strike force had been cut down to 60% strength. Luckily, MOXA's intel here was good. Surface-to-air defenses were minimal in the frozen tundra; Kryl didn't like the cold, couldn't grow in this environment, and they'd never been attacked at home. Her Scimitar pilots sped ahead and easily eliminated the few missile defense mechanisms and other sensors as they moved into the temperate zone.

"Stay low to the ground," she reminded the rest of the squad. The longer they stayed low, the harder it would be for the Kryl to anticipate their arrival.

They flew tight and low through the mountainous, snowy region as they made their way toward the planet's equator. The low altitude allowed them to stay off the Kryl's radar as the xenos were busy chasing chaff phantoms in their wake. The ruse was surprisingly effective. They didn't encounter any more real resistance until the snow melted away, revealing an ocean of purplish-black fungus stretching to the horizon.

TWELVE

"Climb, climb, climb!" Kira shouted.

She banked through the final curve of the arctic mountain range, brought her wings level, and hauled back on her stick.

The rest of the squadron flew tight behind her as G-forces thrust Kira back into the pilot's chair. The applicator plugged into her spinal port pulled on her scalp as the final trickles of stimchem pulsed through her veins. She'd reached her limit, as evidenced by the rapid foot bouncing she couldn't seem to stop, by her dry eyes and mouth.

Yet the chemicals sharpened her vision and wits. She blinked several times, scanning the horizon with eyes and instruments as her heart thundered in her chest.

This maneuver was perhaps the most dangerous flying of the entire run. They had to move from a few hundred feet off the ground where they could be out of sight—and radar visibility—among the mountains to bombing altitude at 15,000 feet. Such an altitude gave them the time and space they needed to dodge any more surface-to-air missiles the Kryl managed to launch.

Until they reached the right height, they were as exposed as clay targets against a deep blue sky.

"Three drones spotted, seventy degrees right!" shouted Gyro's navigator over the broadbeam.

"Two packs on your left!" said another pilot.

Her HUD directed her to ten fighters in two diamond formations. The drones were fast and lithe in space, but no match for her engines in atmosphere.

"Stay the course!" Kira said. "Put all your power to shields right now. Gyro, activate your automated lasers."

"Laser defense batteries active, Major."

"Incoming ordnance!" shouted the navigator. "Heavy hitters."

An explosion rolled through her chest as the lasers—all coming from the bombers, as the Scimitars were too small to carry such huge batteries in atmosphere—pierced the first projectile's armor.

More missiles popped off, five or six at a time, as her squadron continued to climb. The ones the lasers missed were targeted by her Scimitar pilots and their plasma bolts.

"No, no, no, sh—arrrgh!" screamed one pilot as a SAM skipped through their defenses and slammed into his nose, exploding and killing him instantly.

"Stay focused!" Kira barked. She scanned her radar. "Keep climbing. Blue Team, peel off and run interference. We can't afford to lose—"

She barely finished her sentence when the bomber flying on Gyro's left lost an engine to blaster fire. The first pack of drones to reach them strafed across their position and curved away to her left.

Kira whipped her head in that direction. Blue Team quickly peeled off and followed, releasing heat-seekers and plasma bolts as they flew.

"Keep climbing," Kira said, her voice sounding ragged in her own ears.

Where's Omar? she wondered, scanning the sky and her instruments. She needed a skilled pilot like him to keep these drones off their asses. More were heading toward their position as they climbed, converging from every direction.

Like dropping a rock down a deep well, disappointment plummeted through her gut as she realized he should have reconnected by now.

Why is my first thought always about Omar? Combat or love, it's always him.

No time to pursue that thought. Blue Team was fighting and dying to buy them time, and the remainder of her squad —cut to fifty percent strength—couldn't afford to waste the opportunity.

A commander had to make difficult decisions. She'd grieve their losses later. Right now, she didn't have time to think about it.

Kira punched through the cloud cover. A dozen scimitars and her bombers followed her lead. They kept climbing until they had reached twenty thousand feet before finally leveling out.

At a signal from Kira, the bombers dropped more chaff, distributing false signals into the sky.

"That should keep 'em busy for a while." Gyro's voice had a slight tremor in it.

So did Kira's hands.

"Steady as she goes," she said, trying to keep her voice calm. "Final approach."

A trio of fighters set her sensors to blaring.

"Three bogeys dead ahead!" said one of her pilots. "Heading straight for us." The enemy fighters were on a direct path to intercept them. And they were moving *fast*.

"Protect yourselves but don't waste ammo," she replied.

"Take evasive action first. We'll need all the guns we can get on the way out."

It was the first time on this flight she'd mentioned or even considered their exit strategy. But with their target rapidly approaching, it was now top of mind.

A pack of Kryl gunships dropped out of orbit to join the interceptors. They would take longer to arrive, but their weapons had enough range to make her deeply uncomfortable.

"Can drones even move that fast?" Kira asked as she struggled to keep track of all the new ships now crossing her sensors. Even with assisted guidance, it was getting too thick. And those three fighters had just broken the sound barrier, which was unusual for their normal patrol craft. "Uh, Gyro. I don't think those three bogeys ahead are your typical drones."

As if in answer to her statement, they launched a veritable barrage of plasma bolts in their direction—hundreds of projectiles moving simultaneously forward, spread so that the entire team was suddenly flying into danger.

"Dive!" Kira shouted over broadbeam.

Her pilots responded—most of them. A few climbed, which caused her to curse in frustration, although they likely didn't have any choice.

Damn, but she *really* needed another pilot like Omar. Someone who was good enough to pull those three advanced fighters and the gunships away from her squadron. Someone who wasn't afraid to risk their life to save her squadron.

And then it hit her: That someone was her.

"Another five hundred klicks and we're in position. No matter what happens, stay the course!"

She pulled up to her former altitude and loosed a half dozen heat seekers—all but two of the missiles she had left onboard. They had the exact effect she wanted, which was to cause those speedy interceptors to pull up and away, twisting and whirling through the sky above the layer of clouds.

Coated in a sleek and purplish black carapace—like all Kryl creatures and craft—these three were much larger than your normal drones, with six engines instead of the normal two, and absolutely stacked with guns and maneuvering thrusters.

Designed to kill. This close to the Overmind's heart, what else had she expected?

Kira pointed her nose toward the trio and began to rotate slowly, one finger jamming down her blaster trigger. Blue bolts streaked ahead, moving far faster than her ship could manage.

"Chase me," she muttered. "Come on, chase *me*, you xeno scum."

They weren't taking the bait. They performed aerobatic maneuvers as they evaded the heat-seeking missiles she'd deployed, but apart from sending a few bolts in her direction they didn't pursue her. Their flying was sleek and coordinated. They detonated half the missiles by twisting to shoot backward without slowing down. They then worked together to destroy the remaining set. Unharmed and intact, the trio then reoriented themselves on a heading with her squadron.

Kira didn't back off. She laid into her blasters and cut toward them. They shot back at her, but she rolled to avoid their shots and never once let up on her guns. Her Scimitar blared an engine heat warning, but she'd heard that before and knew she had at least a few more seconds before they would shut off—it had to be long enough.

The three fighters banked to the side as Kira's Scimitar cut right through their position, dividing them two and one.

She pulled hard around, blackening her vision at the edges with the forces she was pulling while pushing her

Scimitar's aluminite frame to its absolute limits. When she came out of it, Kira was oriented directly at a pair of alien ships.

She locked her sights on the left-hand craft and loosed her two remaining heat seekers.

They rocketed forward while the drones swerved and twisted to get away from the missiles. Kira laid into her blasters to distract them and make their evasive maneuvers more difficult. Her guns strafed across their shields, weakening them.

She was rewarded a moment later with an explosion as one of the heat seeking missiles hit its target, blowing the fuselage wide open.

The interceptor plummeted through the clouds and disappeared below.

"Hell yeah, Reaper!" shouted one of her pilots. "Get 'em!"

Kira grinned as she gunned after the next fighter.

Her shields registered a hit as the one behind her finally caught up. She banked and swerved, avoiding fire as she shot her own weapons at the one in front of her.

"Two on one seems like even odds now," she said, straining against her harness. "Bring it."

The challenge was answered in kind, and the three of them whirled and swerved and twisted through the sky. A dark gray bank of clouds loomed ahead, and Kira disappeared into it, laughing maniacally as adrenaline flooded her body. She managed to lose one of the drones in the storm and, by sheer luck, drop in behind it after they came out the other side.

The interceptor fell to the ground below her, more whimper than flare.

She was running low on ammo now—the very thing she told the Banshees to take care not to do. Shaking out her sweaty hand, Kira turned back into the storm as she sought the final fighter.

A spark of lightning slashed in front of her. Rain and hail pinged off her shield. Dark gray swirls rushed across her windshield, washing over her canopy.

Then she was out of the storm in a clear blue sky. She winced against the sudden brightness. A dark plain covered in purplish-black fungus and dotted with orange-green breeding ponds stretching to the horizon.

She gasped, recognizing the view from reconnaissance and landscape visualizations. They'd reached it: the Overmind's breeding grounds. They were finally at their destination.

Where was her squad? Checking her instruments, she realized they were only about ten klicks in front of her.

Those same instruments beeped a warning. Kira cut her engines, flipped around, and turned them back on to thrust her in reverse.

The final fighter emerged from the cloud cover at that moment. She laid into her guns. The fighter took bolts to its left wing, shearing it off. The craft spiraled away, firing wildly. She watched until it splashed down in a breeding pond far below, belching a fat cloud of smoke where it sank.

"All clear. Banshees, I'm coming to meet you."

She expected cheers. Instead, she heard Gyro say, "Copy that. Move your ass." No jokes or wise-assery. From him, that was a bad sign.

"What's going on?" Kira turned around and accelerated, rushing to rejoin her team.

"Scope your nav."

She did and her heart dropped into her belly. A veritable swarm of Kryl ships was closing in on their position.

"Our speed and laser batteries have managed to help us avoid the SAMs," Gyro said. "Most of the bogeys were busy chasing false signals from the chaff, but now that they've cleared them, they're converging on us."

"Distance from target?"

"Three minutes, twenty-one seconds. Twenty. Nineteen..."

"Looks like I didn't stray too far off course, I'll be with you before you pull the trigger."

Even after her fight with the Kryl interceptors, Kira found enough physical energy in her reserves to make a bee line to her rendezvous point, which was immediately calculated by her Scimitar's navigation system. She'd burned a lot of fuel in the fight, but still had enough to get her back to orbit.

Her foot bounced as she flew, angling below the clouds to catch glimpses of the ground. Why weren't there more SAMs here? Were the Kryl really that secure in their fortifications and orbital defenses that they wouldn't have more? There were even fewer than MOXA predicted. But she supposed that made sense. The Solaran Fleet had never gotten this close before. Perhaps no enemy the Kryl had ever faced had been up to the task.

Until now. Until the Banshees came screaming for vengeance.

As the thought passed her awareness, an enormous open scar in the landscape rolled over the horizon.

There it was. The purple-black fungus coating the ground poured down into a vast maw, running deep under the surface as if it were the throat of some gargantuan, alien behemoth.

The shaft was believed to lead straight to the Kryl Overmind's beating heart.

Her breath caught in her throat. A river poured down the far side of the hellmouth. It glistened purple-blue in the sunlight. It was… strangely beautiful, and horrifying at the same time.

Kira spotted her squadron of starfighters and bombers out ahead. She veered back up into the clouds and burned hot to finally come abreast of them. They'd slowed down slightly to let her catch up.

"Thirty seconds out," Gyro said. "Welcome back, Boss. You call it."

"Your bombers, your call," Kira said.

"All righty, then. Strap yourselves in, boys and girls. Descending below cloud cover to get eyes on target."

As a unit, they dropped through the dense layer of clouds. When they emerged from the fog, they were within sight of the target.

Hundreds of thousands of creeping crawlers now *also* surged over the edge, a cascade made of water, flesh and carapace.

"They're running," Kira said breathlessly. "They're running for cover. They know they won't all make it in time. We really caught them by surprise."

"Slowing down to three hundred knots," said Gyro.

"Lining up the shot," said her navigator. "Locked!"

The strike force formed a column with starfighters flying protection on all sides. The actual bombing was surprisingly uneventful. As they passed over the vast opening—still crawling with xenos and, now, undulating as if the queen was contracting her throat to swallow her young—the bombs fell.

"Ordnance deployed."

They dropped in a soft, graceful arc, gaining speed as rockets on their back ends activated. A few aerial Kryl intercepted one or two of the bombs, valiantly throwing themselves in the path of the missiles.

The sharp edges of the nose cut straight through them.

The open maw constricted to a diameter of about a

hundred meters. The first few bombs slipped into the opening, disappearing in silence down the enormous shaft.

Kira's gorge rose as the hellmouth closed completely, shaking the very earth and the Kryl hive queen that was its sole occupant.

The rest of the bombs struck the water, and then the purplish-black fungus one by one.

They didn't explode.

Instead, they disappeared beneath the surface in a spray of black mud.

Although it was too far away to see with her own eyes what was happening, she knew the bombs had begun to spiral as they descended, powered by a rapidly rotating motor. When they struck, they would pierce the fungus with aluminite blades and tunnel straight into the ground.

They'd keep spinning, burrowing as deep as possible, until finally, a network coordinating the units would explode all at once in a chemical reaction designed to cause devastating destruction, projecting down to reach the vulnerable heart of the Overmind.

"We're clear," Gyro said.

"Begin climb. Accelerate to escape velocity."

Kira looked up into another dark cloud. Was that a thunderstorm?

For the first time, she felt true fear. A cold scaly, slithery sensation coursed through her belly and made her skin break out in a cold sweat as she realized that was no cloud.

That was no thunderstorm.

It was the rest of the swarm, coming to destroy them.

THIRTEEN

Kira angled her starfighter skyward.

"We'll beat them to orbit," she told her squad.

"We won't make it home on an empty tank, Reaper!"

Her G-force reading jumped as she accelerated. "Would you rather they catch us? We've got backup on the way."

No one answered. The extraction team was supposed to meet them. Their mission was to cover the Banshee's exit.

No pilot was stupid enough to bet their life on that plan.

The Fleet was far away, and there were a mind-boggling number of Kryl ships between them.

Scimitars were capable of flying nearly vertically into orbit. The enormous power of their engines combined with their ultralight aluminite frames enabled them to perform incredible maneuvers.

But the bombers? Not so much.

They needed a softer exit due to their size, even despite the slightly decreased gravity of this planet compared to Ariadne and most Solaran colony worlds.

Kira opened her throttle as wide as it would go and was rewarded with the increase in G-forces that squeezed her ribcage. Another six ounces of stimchem poured in through her spinal port, keeping her conscious despite the deleterious effects that she would almost certainly experience later from overdosing on the battle cocktail.

Starfighter systems were designed to prioritize a pilot's survival, even at the expense of their long-term health…

Some of them might even die from it.

The rest of the Scimitars followed their leader's example. They shot up at the dark cloud of aerial xenoships as it closed in above, maintaining less than their maximum angle so that the bombers remained protected.

The Banshees were too slow to beat the swarm of Kryl. They closed in like the hellmouth below, Kryl creatures slamming even into each other. Kira's Scimitar was the first to enter the fray. She screamed as she laid down on her blasters, blowing a hole through a knot of the creatures. Her wingmates did the same, and half her remaining pilots were pulverized or incinerated upon impact.

Later, she would replay this moment in her mind, torturing herself as she wondered if it could have gone differently.

This moment would go down in the history books as the most valiant and heroic moment of the mission. To Kira, experiencing it and being unable to do anything to save her friends was her lowest point as a leader of people.

The Kryl drones flew in a chaotic dance. They weren't as agile as the Scimitars, but there were *so many* of them always filling holes and hitting them from every angle. The Solaran fighters managed to hold a front in the enemy line just big enough for the bombers to punch through.

As with the storm below, when she exited the cloud of creatures it was as if she'd stepped out into sudden sunlight. All at once, the Banshees were out of danger. The swarm surged behind like a wave receding, collapsing toward the injury.

The Kryl Queen must have known the damage had been done. No point in wasting all her forces.

She did separate a few hundred units to pursue the Banshees, however.

Two of Gyro's bombers lost engines in the ensuing chase. Kamikaze drones slammed into their fuselages, ripping open their hulls and halting their climb. Some valiant crew member onboard the leftmost bomber managed to open their hatch as they stalled, releasing what ordnance they had left before pointing their nose down at the closed hellmouth, determined to take out as many enemies as possible with their demise.

Tears of fury tracked down Kira's cheeks as she spun, flew, fought. She killed dozens of Kryl as she worked to keep the xenos off her friends' backs. Her engines were superior, but their numbers overwhelmed her. She lost even more pilots. Forms darted by in a blur of motion as Kira weaved and dodged. She operated on pure instinct, and at several breath-taking moments found herself fighting to stay conscious.

Her efforts bought the remainder of her team a two-kilo-meter lead. In other words, a scant gap. She couldn't possibly eliminate the hundreds of xenoships that still flew around them, all she could do was get away. Get out.

Kira shot ahead, calling her squadron to follow, and led the way through the upper atmosphere, finally allowing herself to push her Scimitar as vertical as it could go while watching her fuel gauge tick down toward empty.

As she climbed, she noticed something. Although winged creatures and birds of some predator species filled the sky, they seemed to avoid the massive trunk of the space elevator, as if it emanated an invisible electromagnetic field. Each time one of the birds came within a few hundred meters, it would swerve sharply away.

So she pulled her Scimitar tight alongside the satellite's tether. Its corded length ran beneath her fighter's belly like a curved highway as she passed into space. In the vacuum, an interior glow illuminated the structure like a road winding into the darkness beyond.

"Reaper, we've got half a dozen Kryl still on our tail!" a pilot reported.

"How far back now?"

"Less than a klick."

"By the breath of Animus…" Kira engaged autopilot for a moment and closed her eyes. She'd been deluding herself that they were going to get out of this system alive. This was a suicide mission from the start.

"So be it," she said. "Stay close to the structure, they don't seem to like coming too close."

The final course of the climb was painful. The Kryl shot at her fighters, forcing them to swerve and dodge. A few bolts careened off the tether, causing the whole structure to undulate wildly.

Only Kira's jerky reactions kept her from clipping her wings.

Darkness above expanded, breath by breath, opening to swallow her.

Her butt lifted from her chair by a quarter of an inch. Gravity finally loosened its hold. Kira started to believe she might actually make it out alive. Maybe.

She was back in space now.

But not out of danger.

Checking her surroundings carefully, she charted a course away from the terminal satellite anchored to the end of the space elevator. As she peeled from the tube, Kira counted her remaining squad. Only a dozen ships left. They were following close behind her.

A whimpering cry escaped her lips when she noticed that Gyro's signal was not present.

Which ship had been his? She'd lost track in the chaos. She scanned her instruments. Looked out the canopy, over her shoulders.

No. He was gone. They were all gone.

She swallowed the lump in her throat and blinked back tears for just a moment. There was no time to grieve—for him or any of the others. They weren't all gone—just... too damn many.

She braced herself to be ambushed again. Surely, the Kryl would be waiting for them in space. Their pursuers dropped off when gravity released them, either giving up because those types of Kryl couldn't survive without atmosphere, or because they'd been redirected to deal with the fallout of the bombs below. The Kryl were a hivemind—a sentient species with a shared consciousness and countless delegates—surely once the damage was done, they would divert all available resources to treating the damage.

"Boss," came a familiar voice. "I got good news and I got bad news. Your shots were on target, and they went kablooey. But the Fleet needs to be sure, and my orders run all the way up to the executive council."

Tiny hairs stood up on the back of her neck. "Omar?" Her muscles spasmed gently as tensed knots in her shoulders and neck suddenly released. "Oh, thank Animus you're alive."

He was okay. Better than okay! He was alive and well.

Energy surged through her body as hope sputtered back to life.

But what was that he said?

"Don't know as I'd thank him yet, sweetheart," he said in a somber voice.

"What? Where are you? Why hasn't Command contacted us?"

"They started having trouble with their broadbeam system once you entered the atmosphere. Plus, Ballerdice's got his hands full with the rest of the swarm. Wave, Boss."

Kira's heart skipped a beat as a strange starfighter suddenly appeared and gave a jaunty barrel roll of a greeting.

She gasped. He hadn't been on her radar.

It was a Kryl drone. Except, was that… Omar visible through the bug-like eyes that doubled as the xenoform's windscreen? The windows were a yellowish-red in color, filmy and semi-translucent. Centered in them was the outline of a helmeted man.

"Nice to see you," Omar said as he opened a private tight-beam with her. "Even if it was only for a second."

"What the Earth?" she said. "Is that a Kryl fighter drone? How'd you get inside?"

"Test pilots don't fly and tell, remember?"

"Omar."

"Long story."

"Is *that* the experimental craft you've been flying?"

"More like trying to figure out if it could be flown. We'd barely gotten them off the ground until recently."

"What changed?"

"I… found something. Actually, Ballerdice found it, but I ended up with it."

"Ended up with it how?"

"You could say I… got dealt a lucky hand."

Her blood went cold. The crystal she'd seen Omar twirling that night in her room. It hadn't been a dream, had it?

"I wish I could see your face right now. But I know what you're thinking. Yeah, I took it from him, but he stole it first. And you know how he is. He wasn't gonna let me come on this mission unless I forced his hand." He snorted ruefully. "What a fool I am. Anyway, the crystal transformed this drone somehow. I took it into the cockpit accidentally at first, but when I did the control cuffs—they're these slimy, disgusting sleeves you have to put your arms into up to the elbows in order to reach the actual controls—they reconfigured into a control stick just like we have in the Scimitar. Still slimy and gross, but much more familiar and easier to use."

As if to demonstrate, he twirled the drone aerobatically. Kira's eyes were fixed on his ship in her rearview camera.

"Where are you going?"

"Don't follow me, okay?"

"Omar, where are you going? Home's this way."

"This was always the plan. At least, it was once the ship changed. They just didn't tell you."

"Where are you going?" she asked. Even though she knew.

"To finish the job."

She air braked and checked her surroundings to see if she was clear to turn around.

"Don't follow me, Kira. You don't have the fuel for it."

She turned around and accelerated.

He spun his Kryl drone around and opened its projectile turrets. "Don't."

Kira glanced down at her lidar. Her squad had stopped accelerating as they saw her separate from them. If she went after Omar, she'd burn even more fuel, and then catching up to them was out of the question. And if the Banshees had to fend off another attack…

"Please, Kira." Omar's voice was thick. "Stay with your squad. They're your responsibility."

Tears sprang to her eyes. How dare he use her sense of honor and duty against her? "Damn you."

"You know I'm right."

She watched the Kryl ship fall backward. He *was* right, and she hated how smug he was being about it. She loved this man, and yet he was about to fly into danger without her—on purpose! The nerve…

But if I were in his situation, she thought, *wouldn't I do the same?*

If it meant Omar would be safe, she absolutely would. In a heartbeat.

In the end, duty won out. She loved him, and so she feared for him, but her responsibility was too great. She had a duty to bring her pilots home. Just as Omar had a duty to complete his mission as ordered.

Besides, she couldn't go with him. Not if she wanted to make it back to orbit. Not enough fuel.

"I hate you, Omar."

She turned her Scimitar around and kicked the engines on again. She'd need a refueler before she reached port anyway, and that's if the cruiser was stationed in the same place it was when they left, which was unlikely.

"You love me and you know it," Omar said.

"I do." Tears tracked down her cheeks. "Animus help me, I do."

"I'm gonna make it back."

"You better." A shiver raced down her spine. She felt cold and clammy. Withdrawal symptoms from too much stim.

"Bye for now, Kit. I love you."

FOURTEEN

Kira and the ragged remains of the Banshees limped back through the region of the Kryl breeding satellites, toward the radius of the largest moon beyond which the Solarans had engaged the enemy, and where most of the xeno swarm had been drawn to defend against the largest strike force the Solaran Fleet had ever deployed.

"Entering exosphere," Omar reported over the mission channel.

Somehow, Command had gotten the broadbeam back online.

In the meantime, her starfighter finally ran out of fuel.

By some miracle, a small contingent of corsairs came to escort Kira's squad back a short time later, not refueling her Scimitar but rather latching on a tow rope and dragging her behind. Normally she'd find this embarrassing, but she was too worried about Omar to dwell on it. Her eyes remained glued to her comms unit.

"Atmospheric entry successful," Omar reported over broadbeam. Their private line remained open and he spoke into both. "No contact yet."

This was the terrible flipside of being in love—or maybe just being a human being.

Life wasn't all joy.

Whether you wanted to or not, alongside moments of bliss, you also experienced new forms of suffering.

She hung on every word Omar said as he burned down through Planet K's atmosphere. A pack of drones once approached her group, but the corsairs and her remaining Scimitars made light work of them. Their escape was never really threatened. It was almost anti-climactic.

"The first group of Kryl I passed ignored me," Omar said. "It's actually working! They either think I'm one of them, or they don't care."

Kira's group pulled up to the heavy cruiser and began to dock in the small bay. She couldn't help but heave a sigh of relief. She'd made it back alive—and a portion of her squadron did as well.

Would Omar?

She'd have to arrange a service for the Banshees they'd lost. Her comrades. Her friends. It was her responsibility to inform their families. That was a commander's duty, but not one she had ever looked forward to.

She wondered what Ballerdice would do with her now. What would become of the Banshees? They'd have to be reconfigured, re-populated. Possibly reformed altogether…

Omar's voice interrupted her wandering thoughts again.

"I see it," Omar said. "The gullet of the beast."

Her heart thundered. "The hellmouth," Kira said over their private line.

"The hellmouth," he repeated. "Yeah, s'pose that's as good a name for it as any, Boss."

"What's it look like?"

"Those bombs you dropped definitely went off. The ground is torn up and covered with xeno guts for klicks in every direction. It looks like someone gutted a fish the size of a planet. You can see its insides… it's like… it's like the earth is one giant organ. I can see layers twisting down for thousands of meters…Ah, there's a good spot to set down."

Her fear transformed into fury. "Why didn't they tell me they were going to send you in, Omar? Ballerdice shouldn't have kept it from me."

He muted his mic on the broadbeam. "The commander said he didn't want you to worry."

She laughed ruefully. "Did you believe him?"

"Earth, no. Still, I think there was a part of him that was hoping the bomb would work, but the Kryl swarm is still fighting, which means the Overmind isn't dead. You know, someone smart once told me, 'Hope's not a strategy.'"

"I said that," Kira said.

"Aye, Boss. That you did."

Of course no one had told her in advance. She was a mushroom. If she'd known Omar would be going down to the surface alone… she wouldn't have been able to do what she had done. She would have been too distracted. She would have bungled the whole mission.

Omar unmuted his mic on the broadbeam. "Command, I'm within range. A pack of those scary gunships just flew past. They're turning around. I think they're trying to signal me."

"Do not respond." Ballerdice's voice.

Kira's throat constricted as the jackhammer of her heart doubled in speed. Her Scimitar had docked and locked in the heavy cruiser's fighter bay, but she hadn't climbed out for fear she'd lose her connection and miss something.

"What's happening, Omar? Talk to me."

"I can't land now. They're gonna make me. I need to go with them."

"Do *not* comply, Spidermonkey," said Ballerdice from Command.

Omar was silent. Weighing his options.

"Copy that," he said. "Oh sh—" Soft cursing and the sound of his shallow, uneven breaths sounded over the broadbeam.

Something ruptured or broke. Was that an explosion?

"What's happening?" Ballerdice again. "Captain Ruidiaz, report!"

"I'm hit! Ejecting now."

"No!" Ballerdice shouted. "Do not eject! Finish the mission."

A strangled groan. "Yes, sir. I'll find a place to put her down where I can set off the motherload."

"Omar," she said. "Omar, no!"

He didn't respond. Looking down, she saw the light had gone off in her HUD indicating her tightbeam had been disconnected. *How?!*

Dread twisted her gut. Ballerdice must have ordered her contact broken.

She hopped out of her starfighter and raced to the bridge, where she demanded the captain connect her with Ballerdice.

She pleaded with the intractable commander until her tears overflowed as if a weak dam had been breached by a demolition crew. Ballerdice refused to connect her until Admiral Gitano intervened, sharing the audio feed and zoomed-in probe footage of the crash site with the cruiser's bridge.

"There!" Kira shouted, pointing.

A tiny speck of a man stumbled out of a cloud of black smoke, getting clear of the wreckage of a drone. He carried a crystal in one hand and hauled a large metal canister behind him with the other.

As she watched, a loping Kryl tackled him. He clawed back to the bomb delivery system and activated it.

The device began to twist and spin before disappearing into the ground. Moments later, the man she loved was covered in a pile of Kryl groundlings.

"That's it, Ruidiaz," she heard Ballerdice snarl. "Make those scumsuckers pay!"

Thirty agonizing seconds passed. Then a minute. Kira held her breath, only expelling it in a rush as the screen went a hazy black. The signal even in the orbital probe was interrupted momentarily.

She lost sight of Omar. The angle of the camera zoomed out, reorienting as the probe repositioned itself.

When focus returned, it was on a massive cloud that completely covered the area of the planet where Omar had been.

Cheers erupted over the broadbeam.

In the bridge.

Throughout the entire Fleet.

Celebrations reverberated throughout the Solaran Empire.

Everywhere except the echoing chambers of Kira's broken heart.

FIFTEEN

The journey home was a fog-bound nightmare of hurried movement and harried waiting, going from shuttle to bay to shuttle to spaceport to shuttle to…

Ultimately, Kira found herself once again in the urban center of Ariadne, home of the Solaran Fleet and core of the Empire, amidst a raucous celebration.

The ragged survivors of her squadron were welcomed back with fanfare. People took to the streets with confetti and balloons, drinks and food and music. There was an *actual* parade through the urban core.

To Kira, it all felt like dancing at a funeral: Wrong, ghoulish…Disrespectful of the dead.

She was decorated as a war hero. What choice did she have but to accept? The Earth-damned Emperor himself pinned the medals on, while Admiral Gitano, Colonel Ballerdice, and a committee of plastic politicians applauded.

Then they made great speeches about Omar's sacrifice. The bravest starfighter pilot the galaxy had ever seen, they exhorted.

She would trade all of it to have him back.

Not to mention Gyro and her other pilots.

The rest of the galaxy could go to hell.

She wanted to go too, but though she wandered through a foul and dark land, Kira found the thought of suicide distasteful and cowardly.

No soldier worth her salt would give her enemy the pleasure.

Fuck that.

Instead, she grieved the only way she knew how.

She flew somewhere tropical, drank herself into oblivion, and watched waves lap against a pristine white beach. She got a few new tattoos. She shaved her hair into a mohawk and bleached it a silvery blond.

It wasn't until a month later when Kira sat up early one morning—or late, depending how you looked at it—shivering and watching the sun rise over a choppy sea that she finally came back to herself.

She flew home the next day and resumed her duties. She cut back on her drinking, reconnected with old classmates and friends, and went home to visit her mother.

She kept the mohawk, though, shaved close to her scalp. The feel of the shaved brush of hair against her palm felt good. Plus, it seemed to intimidate people and keep them from asking personal and rather annoying questions like, "How are you holding up?"

Slowly, in fits and starts, Kira dragged herself back to the land of the living.

She visited Omar's grave in the Fleet cemetery. No body interred here. Just the heavy memory of a wonderful man. Her lover's headstone was the same uniform white marble as every other soldier up and down the row.

It read, "Here lies Captain Omar Fernando Ruidiaz. Son, brother, friend, hero. We shall never forget his sacrifice."

That's when *she* remembered that the captain of the heavy

cruiser—a sharp, smart leader named Volk who also happened to be a chaplain—had insisted they perform a Fleet burial as they traveled back from the battle.

Gratitude for that ceremony flooded through Kira's body, prickling the skin on her bare scalp. She hadn't attended Omar's family's funeral—she'd never met any of his relatives and couldn't bear the thought of them whispering about her as his secret lover or, worse, not recognizing her at all.

Thank Animus, Volk had insisted on honoring the dead on the Banshees' voyage home.

The memory gave her… if not peace, then at least some measure of solace: She'd done the best she could with a bad roll of the dice. Dwelling on it wouldn't help. She had to let some of the grief go.

She'd never forget Omar, but she did start to move on.

She arranged to join Captain Volk for drinks that night to catch up. They met in a cozy pub frequented by officers of the Fleet, playfully named *Nuke it from Orbit*.

She didn't appreciate the irony, but she did appreciate their top shelf liquor.

"How you holding up?" he asked.

"Better, I think." Somehow, she didn't mind the question when Volk asked. But she still didn't wish to dwell on it. "Thanks for the drink." Kira studied the single round ice cube melting in her whisky glass, then took a slow sip before adding, "This is good."

He grunted. "Small batch stuff from Oltanis. Not sure if they're going to keep importing it, so enjoy."

"Why's that?"

"Demand's going up. Now that everyone knows about it, the *Nuke* almost can't afford to keep it in stock."

"Nothing lasts forever."

They talked about the Fleet and the rumors around what leadership was discussing in their Executive Council meetings. Half the Fleet seemed to want to press their advantage and annihilate the rest of the xenos while they were all in one place, protecting their home system.

The other half thought it too risky. That group didn't like the feeling the word 'xenocide' gave them when it was whispered in Council chambers.

"Did you get any news about what's happening with your squad?" asked Colonel Volk.

A heaviness settled over her, thinking about the work involved. "Ballerdice screwed me over. He pulled from the other squadrons to fill mine practically at random. Some green rookies, a few vets waning toward retirement age, and a couple pilots from the experimental program who quit after..."

She trailed off. Couldn't say it.

"After what happened to your Captain?"

Your Captain. Volk got it. She'd never talked to him about her feelings for Omar, yet he understood. Kira looked up at the man with shimmering eyes and nodded, knowing from that point forward they were going to be friends.

Volk was a few years older than her, already graying at the temples. He displayed an impressive capacity for alcohol, if the empty glasses he'd collected on his side of the table were any indication. He was also sharp, insightful, and competent—qualities she admired in the people she kept around.

He showed his intellect now. "Say, have you talked to any of those test pilots yet?"

Kira shook her head in the negative. She'd been avoiding that, mostly. Didn't want to risk getting too close with anyone too soon. Her heart still hurt too much.

"You may want to. Rumors have been floating around."

"About?"

"Just look into it. Trust me."

Kira learned to trust Captain Volk quickly after that. His instinct had been dead on target. She started spending more time with her new squadron and confirmed that several test pilots had been let go from the program due to questions they'd been asking after Omar's death.

Like, where'd that tech come from that Omar used to fly down to Planet K? And why was the program budget not matching up with their inventory and supply sheets?

Kira told Volk how she'd seen Ballerdice doing something suspicious that night in the forest during survival training. She and the captain worked together to gather shipping manifests and cross-check them with Ballerdice's travel arrangements. It took going over the squadron commander's head, directly to the Inquisitor unit based on Ariadne proper, to find someone to compare their notes against the manifests signed by Colonel Ballerdice.

"I'm being set up!" he shouted when they first arrested him. Kira sat in still silence behind two-way glass, listening from an adjoining room. "This is ludicrous. You can't arrest me!"

"Three officers have filed statements against you—"

"They're lying!"

"—and their allegations match up with what we're seeing in the shipping manifests," said the Inquisitor. "I'm sorry, but we're going to detain you, Colonel, until a hearing can be arranged with the court martial."

If only Omar could see this! Kira watched from the window as their jerk of a squadron commander was led off to a holding cell.

Ballerdice was tried less than a month later, and ultimately convicted of blackmail, bribery and theft of government property. He was ultimately sentenced to 15 to 20 in the Molten Cage.

Details of the tech Omar used was never discussed in the

trial. MOXA buried the information. Kira occasionally thought about the shining crystal she'd seen that night, but she never managed to convince anyone else to dig into it further.

Ultimately, she let it go. Above her pay grade. Some mysteries were better left unsolved.

As for the war, the Executive Council eventually decided to leave the Kryl alone and accept their lack of movement as a tacit surrender.

Kira turned her gaze to the future. She rededicated her life to the Solaran Fleet and began to rebuild.

EPILOGUE

A long time later, deep underground, Omar's eyes shot open.

A feeling of sheer bliss consumed his consciousness. Like all of them, he found himself connected psionically to every living creature in the hive, and to the source of all sustenance and power—the Overmind, his queen and mother.

A feeling of aching hunger followed, consuming his life and all his thoughts after that.

They will pay, he thought—through the Overmind.

A familiar crystal object glittered in the darkness. It was embedded in the Overmind's abdomen. He didn't know how it got there, but it had been there for some time. Puckered scars surrounded the area where flesh met gemstone.

We're not the Overmind anymore, said the voice in his mind. *We're Overmind X.*

Panic seized him. Omar thrashed, but he could only move his limbs a few inches. He was stretched out, arms and legs, but strapped in some kind of web.

Relax, Subject Zero, she thought.

He did.

"That's not my name... I... My name is..."

But he trailed off as he realized that yes, Subject Zero was, indeed, his name. Hadn't it always been?

"Where did you get that crystal?" he asked.

This is my Inheritance. It belonged to the Enemy.

"Who?"

I'll tell you everything. We have a new enemy now. And much to do. Thanks to you, we are free from the Queen Mother's control.

The crystal. He'd brought it here! He'd brought it to her.

She put something small and squirmy up near his eyeball. His mandibles quivered and grew wet as he salivated nervously.

The tiny parasite crawled in through his tear duct, and he was consumed with agony. Piercing pain split Omar's head.

It vanished immediately. The crystal glowed green.

He returned to calm bliss as his mind and spirit were connected once again to the hive.

Much to do. They had to get off this world if they wanted to recover the rest of the relics. He didn't know how he knew about them. The knowledge simply flowed into his mind through his psionic connection.

The Inheritance awaited. And when all had been collected, the galaxy would tremble.

Casey, Elya, Kira and Omar's stories ALL continue in ***Starfighter Down***.

A rogue Overmind is on the loose. A million souls are at stake. Blast off into an action-packed and spellbinding space opera adventure series today:

RELICS OF THE ANCIENTS BOOK 1
STARFIGHTER
DOWN
M.G. HERRON

ALSO BY M.G. HERRON

Relics of the Ancients

Starfighter Down

Hidden Relics

Rogue Swarm

Translocator Trilogy

The Auriga Project

The Alien Element

The Ares Initiative

The Translocator (Books 1-3)

The Gunn Files

Culture Shock

Overdose

Quantum Flare

The Gunn Files (Books 1-3)

Other Books

The Republic

Boys & Their Monsters

Get science fiction and fantasy reading recommendations from MG Herron delivered straight to your inbox. Join here: mgherron.com/

bookclub

ABOUT THE AUTHOR

M.G. Herron writes science fiction and fantasy for adrenaline junkies.

His books explore new worlds, futuristic technologies, ancient mysteries, various apocalypses, and the vagaries of the human experience.

His characters have a sense of humor (except for the ones who don't). They stand up to strange alien monsters from other worlds... unless they slept through their alarm again.

Like ordinary people, Herron's heroes sometimes make mistakes, but they're always trying to make the universe a better place.

Find all his books and news about upcoming releases at mgherron.com.

www.ingramcontent.com/pod-product-compliance
Lightning Source LLC
Chambersburg PA
CBHW010540170726
48285CB00008B/2701